AGAINST ALL ODDS

A SAPPHIC ROMANTIC COMEDY

CARA MALONE

LISBON PRESS

ACKNOWLEDGMENTS

Thank you to my beta reading team, Krys, TeJai and Robin, for the great feedback, criticism and encouragement - you helped make this book something really special!

SAGE

"**D**on't you dare throw the crab cakes!"

The crab cakes were thrown.

A few of them pinged off the cheek of Sage's dad, but most of them left little round grease stains in the wallpaper behind his head. That was the last thing Sage saw before she grabbed her fiancée's hand and dove for cover behind the bar.

"Our families are animals."

"Your sister started it," Rosalie pointed out.

"It was *your* bestie who flung the first pea," Sage shot back.

On the other side of the bar, she could still hear the wedding planner and the venue owner screeching, trying to get people to stop throwing food. They were nearly six months into this, and every step of the wedding planning process had gone pretty much like this.

At least there was booze at this particular fiasco. Sage popped her head above the bar just long enough to snag a bottle of vodka on the counter, then sat down next to Rosalie again, their backs against the bar. She unscrewed the cap, took a long pull and grimaced at the burn of the alcohol down her throat, then handed the bottle to her fiancée.

"Still want to marry me?"

Rosalie took the vodka, managing a much less squeamish swallow. "You can't scare me off with a little mashed potato in my hair."

Sage laughed, running her fingers through Rosalie's soft blonde hair. "Well, it's more than a little."

She did her best to clean the side dish out of Rosalie's hair, then took the bottle back for another swig. Behind them, either their loved ones had run out of food to throw, or they'd actually come to their senses and realized they were grown adults in a very upscale wedding venue, throwing hors d'oeuvres at each other. In any case, things sounded a little calmer, and the wedding planner was shouting for the brides.

"Did they leave?" Sage heard her ask.

"Should we get back out there?" Rosalie wondered.

"Do we have to?"

Rosalie rested her forehead on Sage's shoulder, leaving a small smear of mashed potatoes on her shirt. "How on earth did we get here?"

"Well, one night about a year ago, I met a gorgeous girl..."

2

ROSALIE

ONE YEAR AGO

Rosalie didn't see the pothole in her lane because it was dark, and if she was gonna be totally honest about it, it had more to do with the fact that she was trying to check her phone while she was driving.

She was late and it'd be great if she could text her date to let her know she wasn't ghosting her, but they hadn't exchanged numbers. She at least wanted to check her GPS and figure out *how* late she was.

Way to make a first impression. That was what she was thinking when the front end of her brand-new car dipped and then jolted in the unmistakable sensation of hitting a deep pothole dead-on.

"Fuck!"

She tossed her phone into the passenger seat, the threat of needing her shiny new wheels realigned enough of a warning to pay attention to the road. But the universe wasn't done with her yet.

No sooner had she recovered from the pothole but all

the lights on her dashboard flickered out. She had just enough time to register alarm at this development before the engine died too.

"What the fuck!"

Rosalie was full-blown panicking now, futilely pushing the ignition button and trying to remember her manual signaling gestures. Was it straight arm for turning right? No, up at a ninety-degree angle...

"Fuck it, you gotta get out of the way because I'm coming over," she told any cars that might be behind her as she changed lanes and then pulled onto the shoulder. Thank God her brakes still worked and she at least got to stop where she wanted.

She put the car in park – the very first new car she or anyone else in her family had ever owned, which she just bought four months ago.

The car she still had fifty-six freaking payments left on.

The car that had just stranded her on a busy highway in the dark!

Her heart was hammering in her chest and her mind was racing. *Call a tow truck. I don't know any towing companies. My date's waiting for me. How does a pothole break a whole car?! Why don't they teach you in driver's ed what to do when you break down on the highway?* There were a million thoughts all swirling around in there and none of them were particularly helpful.

The car was rocking back and forth with the force of each vehicle that blew past her at seventy miles an hour, and she hadn't given much thought to where she was pulling over – just that it was necessary. There was a guardrail on the edge of the pavement and the shoulder was narrow. She probably couldn't even get out without worrying about her door... or her body... being sideswiped by traffic.

It seemed like some of them were getting damn close as it was.

It was nine o'clock at night and she was in a black Civic with all its lights out. She might as well have been invisible.

"Fuck, fuck, fuck," she grumbled as she reached with shaking hands into the passenger seat, fumbling for her phone.

She tried to look up a towing company and the internet wouldn't load. "Are you freaking serious? No signal, what is this, the year 2000?"

A lump of frustration formed in her throat as she dialed her best friend. *It's okay, it's not the end of the world,* she assured herself while she listened to the phone ring.

And ring.

And ring.

And then she went to voicemail. Casey wasn't picking up, probably on yet another ill-fated date.

A semi-trailer blew past Rosalie's window, shaking the car, and she swallowed past the lump in her throat. Sure would be a good time to have parents who were reliable or, at the very least, around.

"Okay, you're stranded on the highway with no

internet and no one to call. But you are not helpless so you're going to figure this out."

She climbed awkwardly over the center console and exited on the passenger side, then rooted around in her trunk until she found a couple of road flares in an emergency kit that Casey's dad had given both of them way back when they first started driving. It'd been in the trunk of Rosalie's first car for years and she'd transferred it to the Civic when she bought it.

She was starting to think she would never have to use it, and yet here she was. She figured out how to get the flares lit and put them on the pavement behind and beside her car, nearly pissing her pants when she ventured into the lane to place one, headlights coming at her in the distance.

But when she was done, people were no longer riding the shoulder like they couldn't see her, so that was something.

"Now what?"

She tried Casey again – still no luck.

"Hey, it's Rose. You better be connecting with Mr. Right on a deep and spiritual level because I will not accept any other excuses for not answering your phone right now. I'm broken down on the highway and I need your help."

She made sure her own ringer was on after leaving the voicemail, then tucked her phone into her pocket and decided the only thing to do was go old-fashioned. She'd have to try to flag someone down.

Hopefully not an ax murderer.

"Please, not an ax murderer," she mumbled under her breath as she commenced waving her hands in the air like the damsel in distress she currently was.

She proceeded to have absolutely no luck for ten minutes straight.

At least a hundred cars must have passed her and not a single one so much as slowed down. Maybe she was the one who looked like an ax murderer.

By the time she gave up, her arms were tired, there was a sheen of sweat on her forehead despite the chilly springtime air, and was it her imagination or were her road flares starting to sputter? Soon she was going to be in the dark again, and she sure as hell didn't want to be in or next to the car when it got sideswiped.

She was just climbing over the guardrail when she sensed a vehicle slowing in the right lane.

"Oh, finally, hallelujah!"

She watched it pull over fifty feet or so in front of the Civic, then back up until it was a car's length away. Its hazards started flashing and Rosalie skimmed a hand over her wispy blonde hair, sure it had gone from date-night-ready to windswept-maniac-chic.

The driver's door of the other vehicle popped open and a petite figure appeared, silhouetted in the dark. Small was good, if they were an ax murderer – gave Rosalie a fighting chance, anyway.

The two of them met at Rosalie's hood, and her whole body involuntarily clenched at the woman standing before her.

Chin-length straight hair, a flannel shirt hanging

open with a graphic tee beneath it, jeans ripped at the knees paired with work boots, and a brashness in her expression that immediately drew Rosalie to her.

"Hi." This woman was taking her in just the same way, eyes sweeping over Rosalie, sizing her up like they had all the time in the world and there weren't eighty-ton semi-trucks blasting past them just feet away.

"Thanks for stopping. I feel like I've been out here forever." She licked her lips and added, "I'm Rosalie."

"Sage," her hero answered, holding out a hand.

It was warm and soft, and not shaking like Rosalie's hand, her body pulsing with adrenaline.

"You're in luck, I'm a mechanic," Sage said, nodding toward the Civic. "Do you know what the problem is?"

"Not a damn clue." Rosalie explained about the pothole, the flickering lights, the engine failure. Once she started talking, the adrenaline took over and she couldn't seem to stop. "I've never broken down before and this car is basically brand-new and I can't believe you're a mechanic. Are you also an ax murderer, by any chance?"

Sage chuckled, the rumbly sound doing something in Rosalie's own chest.

"What if I said no, but only because the ax isn't my weapon of choice?" She delivered the line dead-pan, then turned to the Civic. "Mind if I take a look under the hood?"

"Be my guest."

Rosalie stood by the guardrail between their two cars while Sage popped the hood and bent over it. Her jeans tightened slightly against her ass when she bent forward like that, and in spite of her concern about the car, Rosalie couldn't help appreciating the view.

It didn't take Sage long to turn back around, holding up a fistful of something. "Found the problem."

"I don't know anything about cars, but I don't think they're supposed to be stuffed with... what is that?" Rosalie asked, coming closer.

"Looks like woodchips... foam... cotton... Let me take a wild guess that you park in a garage in the winter."

"A car port."

"With a couch or something in it?"

"One of my neighbors put one in his spot, said he was gonna coordinate with the trash service to get rid of it but he never did."

Sage tossed the handful of fluff in the grass over the guardrail. "You had mice nesting on your engine block, probably all winter. While they were in there, they took the liberty to chew on some of your tasty wiring."

"Bastards."

"They were just trying to survive. Anyway, my guess is when you hit the pothole, it jostled the wires *just right* and broke a vital connection. You could get it fixed at the dealership, but your warranty isn't gonna cover this," Sage said. "Or you could come over to my garage and I could fix it for you tonight."

"Seriously?"

"It's an easy repair."

"And then you'll murder me with your weapon of choice?"

Sage laughed. It was deep and throaty, not something

you'd traditionally label an attractive laugh, but it was so genuine that Rosalie felt herself falling just a little bit in love. Or maybe it was just the gratitude talking.

Sage held out her hand again, pinkie extended. "Pinkie promise, I will not murder you, ax or otherwise, if you extend me the same courtesy."

"Deal." Their little fingers still interlocked, Rosalie met Sage's gaze and asked, "How do we get my car to your garage?"

3

SAGE

"So, do you stop for all the girls you see broken down on the highway?"

They were in Sage's garage – not a mechanic's shop but the detached garage behind her parents' house that she'd turned into a workshop years ago. It was late, the house lights were off, and Sage had just finished clearing all the mouse bedding out of Rosalie's engine compartment.

Rosalie was perched on a stool next to the right wheel well, watching her work. Distracting the hell out of Sage with those heather-gray eyes ringed with a darker shade of granite.

"It's not all that common these days," Sage said. "You got unlucky breaking down in a dead zone. Or I got lucky."

She hoped Rosalie wouldn't notice that she had a tendency to pause before responding longer than most people. She'd been doing it since they met so chances were that ship had sailed. It didn't happen all the time, but as luck would have it, today was one of those brain foggy days – and it didn't help that she was trying to juggle the car repair and a conversation with a beautiful woman.

Thankfully, if Rosalie noticed, she didn't mention it.

She was watching intently as Sage inspected the wires closest to where the mice had made their nest. Rosalie leaned forward on her stool, her blonde hair sliding over her shoulders like a waterfall.

"Aha." Sage slipped one finger underneath a nibbled wire, lifting it up for Rosalie to see.

"No! Is that going to be expensive to fix?"

Sage suppressed a chuckle. "Nah, I can swap out the wires in a few minutes, not a big deal."

In the time it took to call a tow truck and drive with Rosalie to her garage, Sage had gotten surprisingly attached to her. Or at least curious about her. The woman was strikingly beautiful, that was for sure, and she seemed to glow with energy, even when she was distressed and broken down on the side of the highway.

Sage had been secretly hoping that whatever was wrong with Rosalie's car, it would take a while to fix.

She found two more chewed wires, one entirely severed, but nothing that would take more than ten minutes to swap out. Damn the luck.

"Well, I'm paying you for the parts as well as your labor," Rosalie insisted. "I still can't believe you didn't let me pay the tow truck driver."

"He's a friend from mechanic school," Sage shrugged.

She went to her workbench to look for replacement wires, brushing past Rosalie in the tight space. Her hair smelled like her namesake.

"Still, we called him out at nine o'clock at night."

"He's used to it... People need tows at all hours." She pulled a spool of wire out of a toolbox and squeezed past Rosalie a second time. She was wearing a gauzy, flowy dress that accentuated all her curves and Sage had laid a towel down on her stool to protect it before she'd allowed Rosalie to sit. "Besides, we have a symbiotic relationship. He tows people here, I give clients with beater cars his business card."

"How long have you been a mechanic?"

"About eight years." She scoffed and added, "I should probably be out of my parents' garage by now, shouldn't I?"

"I don't see anything wrong with this setup."

Rosalie looked around, and Sage saw the space through her eyes. Or what she *thought* Rosalie was seeing, her inner therapist interjected. The tool bench was cluttered and disorganized. There were grease stains on the floor. The space lacked the tools that a professional garage would have, like a lift and welding equipment.

"I do okay," Sage allowed, reluctantly. "What about you? What do you do?"

"I'm a journalist. I write for the Hickory Harbor Gazette." Rosalie shifted on her stool. "Mostly local interest stuff, events in the area and things like that."

"I haven't read a paper in probably a decade," Sage

said, bent over the engine compartment. It didn't occur to her that was probably a rude thing to say until the words were already out of her mouth.

She hazarded a glance at Rosalie, who just nodded.

"Most people haven't," she agreed. "The vast majority of our readership is online."

She was so open, not an ounce of defensiveness in her response, not a shred of judgment in her gaze when she looked around Sage's garage, or listened to her struggling to find her words, or got unintentionally insulted. When was the last time Sage met someone like that? Probably not since she frequented playgrounds and drank from juice boxes.

Sage cleared her throat. "It'll just take me a minute to swap out this wiring and then you can be on your way to... wherever it was you were going before you broke down."

"Oh shit!"

Sage straightened up so fast she clipped the crown of her head on the car hood, suppressing a hiss of pain. "What?"

Rosalie's cheeks colored the most beautiful coral. "I ghosted someone tonight. I totally forgot about her until this minute."

Sage's heart climbed into her throat, a place it really had no business being since all she was doing was helping a stranger with car trouble. She had no right to feel jealous, but still she had to ask, "Someone you're seeing?"

"First date," Rosalie explained, then laughed. "And also the last, considering I didn't show up."

Phew. Sage's heart found its way back to her chest where it belonged and she tried to ignore how much she liked this girl. She had no reason to expect this to go any further than a simple favor, and history had taught her to pay attention to that instinct.

Nothing good ever came from expectations, planning, thinking too far ahead.

"It wasn't your fault," she pointed out. "You could call her, explain what happened."

Rosalie shook her head. "I don't have her number – it was a blind date sort of arrangement, friend of a coworker. I wasn't super enthusiastic about the idea in the first place."

"And neither were the mice, apparently."

Rosalie laughed, the sound bouncing off the walls of the garage and brightening the grimy space. "It wasn't meant to be."

But this was, Sage mused, and before she could help herself, she said, "You know, I hardly ever drive that route at this time of night. The only reason I was there tonight was my sister Willow finally let me come over and take the snow chains off her car."

"Huh, maybe fate was at work tonight after all." Rosalie was smiling at Sage and it damn near made her hit her head on the hood again when she finished her work.

"Let's give it a try," she said, extending her hand to help Rosalie down from her stool. Her hand was manicured, nails short and rounded and painted a soft pink.

There was not a single thing about her that wasn't perfect, as far as Sage could tell.

Rosalie sat down behind the wheel and crossed her fingers. "Here goes nothing."

She pushed the ignition button and for a second, Sage hoped nothing would happen – except that Rosalie would have to spend more time with her while she fixed the car.

But the headlights splashed on, the dashboard lit up and the engine roared to life. And Rosalie beamed up at her. "You're a genius!"

"It was easy," Sage said, looking at her scuffed sneakers.

"Maybe, but it means a lot to me." Rosalie left the car running and got out. Sage was standing right beside her door and now they were face to face, nothing between them but the tension in the air. "Are you sure I can't pay you?"

"I'd be a little offended if you did. I shouldn't get paid to have fun like this."

"Says who?"

"Capitalism?" Sage wasn't really sure, it was just a gut feeling. "Are you gonna go see if your blind date waited for you?"

"No, I'm sure she's gone by now," Rosalie said. "It's late, I think I'll just go home."

"Okay."

Weak answer, Sage chastised herself.

Rosalie was lingering, waiting for something, but she couldn't seem to convince herself to go for it. It was easier when there was an engine block between them, something for Sage to fiddle with.

"I should get out of your hair…"

Rosalie gave her a questioning look and Sage just nodded. "Your car's good to go, I'm sure you don't want to spend any more time in a dingy garage."

"You might be surprised," Rosalie said with a furtive smile. Then she sank back down in the driver's seat. She put on her seatbelt and pulled the door closed, then rolled the window down. "Thanks again for your help. I was really panicking."

"No problem, it was easy."

Sage watched the brake lights paint the back wall of the garage red and stepped back as the car started to roll forward. Meeting Rosalie had been the perfect end to an otherwise unremarkable day, but it was over now. She was too chicken to tell Rosalie how much fun she'd had tonight.

All she did was fix a few wires. What kind of weirdo starts gushing after something like that?

The brake lights came on again, the Civic halfway out of the little single-bay garage, and Rosalie stuck her head out the window. Sage's heart jumped right back into her throat.

"Forget something?"

"Yeah," she smiled, her hands on the doorframe, her breasts resting on top of her hands and pushing up to strain the bounds of her bra. "Look, I know you were just helping me out and maybe you don't want anything more to do with me, but you just did all that for free…" Rosalie hopped out of the car and came back to where Sage stood. "I want to at least thank you, if you won't allow me to pay you."

Sage opened her mouth, shocked, and Rosalie's eyes went wide.

"Oh my God, not like *that!*" She smacked Sage's shoulder. "Have you heard of the Blue Whale Festival?"

"Is it something I could look up on Urban Dictionary?" Sage asked, eyebrows wrinkled.

"Get your head out of the gutter," Rosalie laughed.

"You're the one who put it there," Sage pointed out. "What is the Blue Whale Festival?"

"It's new. This is their first year but they're hoping to make it an annual thing," Rosalie explained. "It's to fundraise for conservation, but there's going to be all kinds of food and activities down at the pier next weekend. I have to cover the event for the Gazette, and I was wondering... do you wanna go with me?"

"As..."

"As my date," she confirmed.

Sage grinned. "Yeah, okay."

Rosalie was glowing again as she rose onto her tiptoes and planted a quick kiss on Sage's cheek – one that left her wanting so much more as she watched her hop back in her car and disappear into the night.

4

SAGE

Sage was admiring Rosalie over the top of an enormous candy apple covered in everything from sprinkles to whole gummy bears. The thing looked like it had been dropped and rolled around on a daycare carpet, but the look of absolute bliss on Rosalie's face was so much better.

She was savoring that damn thing with every ounce of her being. And cracking up the whole time because she was struggling to even get her teeth around it.

"That apple too much for you to handle?" Sage teased.

"You wanna help me with it?" Rosalie held it out for her.

Sage took a bite, winding up with sticky candy glaze on the tip of her nose. "Do you always eat like this?"

They'd been at the Blue Whale Festival for about an hour now and she'd watched Rosalie sample every single thing offered to her, from a deep-fried pickle to loaded fish n' chips, a blooming onion, and now this monstrosity that used to be fruit.

"When in Rome," Rosalie shrugged, then pointed at the press badge she wore on her shirt. "You don't think I wore this as a fashion statement, do you?"

"I figured you wore it to impress me."

She smiled. "That too, but I get lots of samples if people know I might include them in my write-up of the festival. And of course I need to be fair, so I need to try everything." She took another bite of candy apple then wiggled it, with great effort, into the cellophane bag the vendor had given her. "But I absolutely will go to sleep with a stomachache tonight."

"Let's do something that doesn't involve food next," Sage suggested.

The festival was a big street fair stretching the length of Hickory Harbor's largest pier. There were a ton of food trucks, all donating part of their proceeds to the cause, and also craftspeople and artists – a lot of them with whale-themed merch – plus a few music stages, some carnival games, and the *pièce de résistance,* Wally.

Wally was a full-scale inflatable model of a blue whale on loan from the conservation group that organized the event. He was eighty feet long and was currently monopolizing a large portion of the beach.

"And the best part?" Rosalie excitedly informed Sage as they headed in that direction. "You can go inside!"

"Inside the whale?" Sage sputtered a laugh.

"Yeah, he's anatomically labeled in there and everything so you can basically go all the way through his digestive system."

"You really know how to show a girl a good first date," Sage said. "I get to be whale poop with you? That blind date you stood up will never know what a good thing she's missing out on."

"I'm a laugh a minute," Rosalie said with a sarcastic smirk, but Sage wasn't disagreeing. This was by far the most fun she'd had in a long time, even if the rapid-fire barrage of flavors and activities and sounds and lights was a little disorienting.

"No food inside the whale," one of the staffers said when they got to the beach. "No shoes, either."

They kicked off their shoes in the sand, where a lot of other people had already done the same, and Rosalie carefully set down her candy apple on top of her sandals, then took Sage's hand. She was so brazen, just taking whatever she wanted and assuming she wouldn't be rebuffed, rejected, emotionally skewered.

Sage was in awe of her.

"You ready?" Rosalie was looking at her with questioning eyes, and Sage realized her brain had short-circuited when Rosalie threaded their fingers together.

"Yeah. Important question – which end are we going in?"

Rosalie laughed. "The mouth, I hope."

Wally the inflatable blue whale was exactly as promised. The realism kind of fell apart at the entrance, which looked less like a whale's mouth and more like the entrance to a particularly long and strange bouncy castle, but inside, it was quiet and dark and warm, and calm blanketed Sage as the chaos of the festival faded away.

"So this is how Pinocchio and Geppetto felt," she said, still holding Rosalie's hand as they inched forward.

"That was a sperm whale, actually."

"I love a woman who knows her whales."

Rosalie laughed again, the trill filling the space just like it had filled Sage's garage the other night. It was lovely and Sage would have stayed forever if there wasn't a line of people waiting to walk through Wally.

"I wouldn't have known that off the top of my head, but it came up when I told a coworker I was covering this festival," Rosalie shrugged. "We googled it."

"Shh, don't spoil the illusion."

Rosalie looked at her, those eyes ringed in two different shades of gray reflecting the glow-in-the-dark organs someone had painted on the inner walls of the inflatable whale. Sage had a strong urge to kiss her, right there between the heart and the stomach.

And then a small child bumped into her from behind and she realized they no longer had Wally all to themselves.

"Come on, I'll win you a souvenir Wally over at the darts booth," she said, urging Rosalie forward.

"That confident in your dart game, huh?"

"I dabble."

"What a coincidence, so do I."

Sage shot her a wry smile, even though she wasn't sure if Rosalie could see it in this whale-innards lighting. "Care to make it interesting?"

"Always."

5

ROSALIE

S age was not kidding when she said she was confident in her dart game.

Rosalie *may* have been exaggerating when she said she dabbled. What she really meant was that she was aware of the rules of the game, and that she played a couple times in college until an RA found out that Casey's boyfriend had installed a dartboard in his dorm room and made him take it down.

She definitely had not been expecting Sage to mop the floor with her, which she did for three consecutive games.

"I haven't seen that many bullseyes since I covered last year's 4H winners," she said as the attendant handed Sage a small blue whale stuffed animal.

"I told you I dabble."

"I guess that means different things in our worlds."

Sage handed her the stuffed animal, cute and soft, with beans in its belly. "Should I have let you win? Some-

24

times I'm not the best at the more subtle end of social cues."

Rosalie wrinkled her brow. "Hell no. If you're good at darts, be good at darts. Don't change yourself for my sake."

Sage stood a little taller, then nodded at the whale. "You like it?"

"I love it," Rosalie said quickly. "I'm gonna bring it in and put it on my desk at work so everybody there knows who gets the best assignments." She winked. "And has the best assistant helping me scope things out."

"Oh yeah, does that mean I'm gonna get on the byline?"

"Come with me and listen to the Beach Boys cover band that's supposed to start in a couple minutes and we'll talk."

The band was good, and the stage area was crowded. The sun was starting to set and the air got chilly even with all those people around. Rosalie didn't need much encouragement to use it as an excuse to snuggle up to Sage – for one thing, she smelled like warm cider and the cardigan she was wearing looked very inviting. For another, Rosalie really was freezing her butt off.

She'd chosen another light, flowy dress – one of dozens in her closet, perhaps a bit early in the season, but she'd picked it because she'd caught Sage looking sideways at her body a couple of times the other day in the garage, and she'd really liked that feeling.

When Rosalie bumped up against Sage's shoulder, then rested her body there, Sage took the cue. She wrapped her arm around her and their hips came together as they swayed to "Don't Worry Baby."

"Cold?" Sage asked, her voice vibrating in Rosalie's ear.

"A little."

Sage opened her sweater and enveloped Rosalie in it, the warmth of her body immediately radiating through the gauzy dress.

"You *are* cold," Sage tutted, wrapping her arms more tightly around her. She was only an inch or two taller than Rosalie, probably couldn't see the stage at all now, but Rosalie wasn't really looking at the band anymore either.

"I like you," she confessed, leaning back against Sage's chest.

"Even though I'm not the most eloquent conversationalist?"

"I don't know what you mean."

"And even though I think your taste in fair food is questionable?"

"I also think it's questionable," Rosalie shrugged. "But it's not every day someone offers you a gummy-bear-covered apple."

Sage's cheek shifted against the side of Rosalie's head as she grinned. "Even though I kicked your butt at darts?"

"That just means I need a rematch... and to practice a hell of a lot more."

"There's a dartboard in my garage."

"Perfect."

The song ended and the crowd shifted, people

coming and going to other parts of the festival. The band played the opening instrumental notes to "Wouldn't It Be Nice," and Sage whispered in Rosalie's ear, "I like you too."

Blood rushed into her cheeks, her head all tingly and warm with the vibration of Sage's words. And then she turned, and just as the lead singer came in strong with the lyrics, their lips met in a crescendo of their own.

6

SAGE

The first few months with Rosalie were a dream come true – one that Sage had never dared allow herself to have.

It seemed so far beyond the realm of possibility that to imagine it would only be a form of self-torture. But there she was, rapidly falling in love with the most perfect, beautiful, fun, understanding and interesting woman she'd ever met.

She was waiting for the other shoe to drop at any moment, but it never did.

They took each other to their favorite restaurants. Sage taught Rosalie how to change a tire and jump a dead battery. Rosalie took Sage to the newspaper offices and gave her the grand tour. They practiced their dart game (Sage continued to wipe the board with Rosalie, and feel mildly guilty about it).

And they moved fast.

It was hard not to, when every cell in her body was

telling her that this woman was made for her, her other half, her perfect complement. And, you know, hot as hell to boot.

They were at Rosalie's apartment the first time they made love.

It wasn't just sex, or even a good old wanton fucking. They'd only been dating for a week but the tension between them was practically palpable. Even Sage, with her limited experience with dating, knew better than to confess her feelings already, but she couldn't help telling the truth with her body.

They peeled each other's clothes off, layer by layer, savoring the experience. Rosalie was hardly ever in anything other than a dress, and tonight she had on cute little Mary Jane heels and a matching belt with a little leather bow at her waist. She paid so much attention to detail in everything from her appearance to the date ideas she came up with, and Sage wanted to devote just as much attention to stripping her bare.

Kissing every inch of her.

Exploring her curves.

Drinking her in.

Beneath the dress, Rosalie wore a satin bra and panty set in blush pink, just a shade or two darker than her fair skin. She kept the Mary Janes on as she stepped out of the panties, and Sage's heart rate cranked up until she could hear it.

"Your turn," Rosalie said as she let the panties dangle from one finger before dropping them to the floor and stepping forward. She put her hands on Sage's belt, popping the clasp and pulling her hips hungrily toward her in the same motion.

Sage pulled her long-sleeve t-shirt over her head, then let Rosalie slide her fingers up the faint ridges of her ribs and beneath the band of her bra. She peeled it up and over too, tossing it aside, then dropped to her knees to liberate Sage from her pants as well.

When she was naked and pulsing with need and practically salivating at the sight of Rosalie on her knees before her, Sage ran her hands through Rosalie's soft blonde hair, down the side of her face and underneath her chin. She lifted her head till Rosalie was looking up at her.

Taste me.

I want to see you come on my hand.

You're the most perfect woman alive.

She could have said any of those things. They were all on the tip of her tongue. Hell, even something cheesy like *If I said you had a beautiful body, would you hold it against me?* would have been better than what she actually said.

Because what she actually said killed the moment dead.

"I need to tell you something."

Rosalie's brow furrowed. "Is everything okay?"

Sage took her hand and pulled her to her feet. "I just think I need to tell you this before things go any further."

She led Rosalie to the foot of the bed to sit down and noticed her eyes were wide with alarm. "You're scaring me. You're not like, married or something, are you?"

Sage couldn't help snorting at the idea. "No, definitely not."

She took a deep breath. She'd only had to say this a couple of times in the past decade, and usually it was to someone whose opinion didn't matter this much to her, like a doctor or the members of her therapy group.

This time, she didn't know what to expect. Rosalie could decide to cut and run... and Sage wanted to give her that option before they had sex... before Sage fell completely and hopelessly in love with her.

"Please don't keep me in suspense," Rosalie prodded. "My mind's coming up with all kinds of creatively horrible things over here. Did you hear the news story about the woman who pretended to be six and got adopted by an unsuspecting couple?"

"You think I want you to adopt me?"

Rosalie laughed, and then Sage did too. It brought her heart rate down and gave her space to breathe as she told Rosalie what she needed to know.

"I have schizophrenia."

She looked into Rosalie's eyes, trying to spot the awful stereotypes whizzing by in her brain, the Hollywood dramatizations and the violent incidents that always got blown up in the media. Then she rushed to explain.

"I got diagnosed about ten years ago and I'm managing my symptoms with medication and therapy, but it is something that I actively deal with," she said all in one breath. It was a well-rehearsed speech so she thankfully didn't struggle through it, but that didn't make it any easier to say to the girl of her dreams. "I wanted you to know so that you could... you know, leave. Or, well, this is your apartment, so I guess I–"

"Sage." Rosalie took her hand, stilling her racing thoughts. "I'm not leaving, and I don't want you to."

"You don't?"

"No. I have to confess, though, I don't know much about schizophrenia, so I might need you to explain it some more later."

"Later?"

Rosalie's mouth curved up in a half smile and her eyes traced down Sage's body, settling on her dark brown nipples and small, pert breasts. "We were in the middle of something I've been looking forward to. Do you want to finish that first, then talk?"

"You still want to?" Sage's body reacted immediately to the idea, revving back into high gear. "You're not scared?"

"Of you?"

Sage nodded. "Some people are, after they hear that word."

"Well, those people are ignorant. I'm not scared."

I am, Sage thought, but she shoved the trepidation aside and embraced Rosalie instead, determined to savor this moment... just in case she only got one chance.

She pinned Rosalie's shoulders to the bed, crawling on top of her and showering her in kisses. She tasted the sweetness on her lips, discovered the little heart-shaped mole on the underside of Rosalie's left breast, found out the insides of her thighs were delightfully ticklish.

"Stop, stop," Rosalie gasped after a few seconds of Sage exploiting that particular weakness. She was out of breath and squirming, and holding Sage tight all at the same time.

Could she have it all?

It never seemed possible, and yet here *it* was, splayed out before her, absolute perfection in a five-foot-five package. And then Rosalie threw her legs around Sage's hips, tugging her body closer, and she forgot all about hopes and dreams and impossible goals because she was living it.

And the sex? Fucking incredible.

The way Rosalie's mouth felt – not just on the usual spots but even when she was just planting a kiss on Sage's shoulder – was enough to give her a full-body orgasm. Every brush of her fingers over Sage's skin, every whisper of her breath standing Sage's fine hairs on end was heavenly.

If they had made love that first night and then Sage died at the age of twenty-seven, she wouldn't have minded too much... as long as she got to meet up with Rosalie wherever she ended up next.

7

ROSALIE

It was true that Sage's diagnosis didn't scare Rosalie, but the reporter in her recognized how little she knew about schizophrenia, so after that night, she went out and got educated.

She read books, watched YouTube videos, and asked Sage questions here and there, trying not to be annoying with them.

"You don't have to tiptoe around this subject," Sage told her one afternoon when her parents were both at work and they were taking the opportunity to have lunch – naked – at her place.

They'd just fucked fast and hard in Sage's bedroom, a fantasy she'd been cultivating for years and which she told Rosalie had just been blown out of the water by the real experience. They got hungry, and they'd wandered down to the kitchen to raid the fridge without bothering to put on clothes. While they stood at the counter wolfing down turkey sandwiches, Rosalie had started thinking

34

about the fact that Sage lived at home, wondering if it had anything to do with her mental health.

"So, why do you... I mean... do you like living with your folks?" The question was awkward, and it had already started to come out of her mouth before she realized how rude it was and had attempted to reverse course.

"There's not really a polite way to ask somebody why they still live at home, you know," Sage said, but her tone was lighthearted. She laughed when she saw the stricken look on Rosalie's face and added, "It's fine, you're not gonna offend me over something that's just the truth. Yes, I live with my parents. Ask what you want to ask."

She was going to force Rosalie to put it to words, but after a couple weeks of skirting around various mental health topics, it was probably time to just be blunt with each other.

"Is it because of your condition?"

"No." Sage took a bite of her sandwich. "It was at first. I was living in an apartment with some friends the first time I had psychosis. It took a while to figure out what was wrong, but I wound up getting hospitalized and that's when they diagnosed me. I wasn't really prepared to go back to living on my own, and unlike you, my friends at the time weren't so understanding. They didn't really want me back."

"Assholes."

"It wasn't totally their fault," Sage said. "We were all young, immature, uninformed."

"Are you still friends with them?"

A shadow fell over Sage's features and she shook her head. "Anyway, living with my parents was the right move back then, helped me adjust and find a new normal." She shrugged. "I never left because now I've got my repair shop out back and... I don't know, never had much reason to move out. I do pay rent, though – I'm not freeloading."

"That's not what I was getting at," Rosalie said. "I was mostly wondering how you'd feel about living with a partner someday."

Sage's lips turned up in a wry smile. "A partner?"

"Me," Rosalie rolled her eyes. "I mean, not tomorrow or anything – we've only been going out a few weeks. But eventually?"

"I would love that." Sage had a way of sounding so earnest, looking into Rosalie's soul with her warm brown eyes and making her believe she was the only other woman in the world.

In reality, they were *not* the only two people in the world, and they were rudely reminded of that fact when a key was inserted in the lock at the back door and suddenly Sage's eyes went wide.

"Dad's home, get upstairs!"

She shoved the naked Rosalie toward the kitchen doorway and the two of them bolted up the stairs and back into Sage's bedroom. Rosalie hadn't actually met Sage's parents yet, and she definitely did not want to do it in the nude. Her heart was hammering by the time Sage slammed her bedroom door shut, and they heard her dad shout, "Why ya slamming doors? Hey, what's with this mess in the kitchen?"

They'd left their sandwich-making supplies spread out across the counter, fully intending to clean it all up when they were done eating. Now, though, Sage reached over and clicked the lock on the door, then collapsed into Rosalie's arms in a fit of laughter.

'Eventually' turned out to be a lot faster than they were expecting, when it came to moving in together.

Neither of them had ever lived with a romantic partner, although they'd talked about it a number of times after that day in Sage's kitchen. What kind of apartment they'd like, whether it should allow pets, how much the two of them could afford. Rosalie loved daydreaming about it, and her little studio was a bit of a dump, but her lease wasn't up for eight more months and Sage couldn't squeeze into that little place with her anyway, so it was all strictly hypothetical.

Until one day she came home from the newspaper offices to find an eviction notice duct taped to her door.

That alone was alarming – she'd never been late on her rent, never so much as had a neighbor bang on the wall to tell her to pipe down.

Further, according to the notice, she had only twenty-four hours to pack up and get out.

But the most alarming thing was the information *on* the eviction notice.

"The reason for this eviction is a large-diameter sinkhole that was identified beneath the building during a routine inspection," Rosalie read to Sage as soon as she got her on the phone. "Holy fucking shit!"

"You can't stay there."

"They're not going to let me."

"No, I mean tonight," Sage said. "Come to my house. Or I'll come over there and help you pack first, and then we'll come back here."

By the time Sage arrived in her truck with some flattened packing boxes in the back, the police had arrived and were beginning to string up caution tape all around the building.

"I guess the landlord thought the eviction notices were good enough, but the building inspector begged to differ," Rosalie told her. "They're giving me an hour to go in and pack my stuff."

"Because the sinkhole has graciously agreed not to swallow the building for another hour?" Sage asked.

"I don't know, but there's stuff in there that I've had since I was little – I have to take my chances to get it. At least the apartment came furnished so I don't have to worry about moving any big stuff."

"I'll go with you," Sage said, taking her hand. "Two people can pack faster than one."

"Make that three," Rosalie's best friend, Casey, said as she joined them on the front lawn. Rosalie had called her right after Sage, and Casey had offered her couch but

Sage's bed was a far more attractive offer. Casey said she'd at least come help them pack.

So that was how Rosalie lost her apartment and met Sage's parents for the first time that night, and how Sage met Rosalie's best friend. All because of a sinkhole that the police could not tell them anything about – the size, how much danger it really was, how long it might have been there.

Rosalie curled up next to Sage in her twin-size bed that night, all of her belongings in cardboard boxes cluttering up Sage's garage. She was acutely aware of the fact that Sage's parents slept just on the other side of the wall, and there was a slight breeze where her backside hung slightly off the narrow bed, but in spite of all that, being tucked into Sage's embrace felt good.

It felt right, actually, like she was home.

Well, not literally.

"What do you think of apartment hunting with me in the morning?" she whispered, so as not to wake Sage's parents. "I know it's a lot sooner than we were planning, we've only been together two months, but–"

"I think it's perfect." Sage kissed her forehead. "Besides, I can't make love to you when my parents might be able to hear, so the sooner the better."

Rosalie laughed. "I mean, I could get another studio without a sinkhole feature if you're not ready to move in with me."

"Oh, I'm ready. The real question is, are you ready for me?" Despite her own objections, Sage's hand found Rosalie's thigh beneath the covers. It at once aroused and tickled her when Sage's fingertips feathered their way over her skin, and she squirmed under her touch.

"Stop or I'll scream," Rosalie giggled, and Sage sank her fingernails into Rosalie's thigh.

"I am very much looking forward to making you scream at full volume."

Her hand retreated and they went back to snuggling. Rosalie nuzzled into the curve of Sage's neck, inhaling her scent. "I guess we should look for a standalone then, or at least something with thick walls."

"Something with a garage, or near a real mechanics' garage with a stall I could rent out..." Sage dreamed aloud as she drifted off.

It took them two weeks to find the perfect apartment, in a nice area not far from the pier, with plenty of space for the two of them but within their budget. It had big, south-facing windows in the bedroom and exposed brick in the living area and kitchen, giving it an artist's loft vibe. Rosalie's commute to the newspaper offices was a lot shorter, and there actually were a couple of mechanics' garages nearby.

Sage went down and introduced herself to the owners of both places during their first week in the apartment, just to feel them out, but one didn't have any stalls open and the other gave her sticker shock when he told her the rent.

"It's fine, I don't think I'm ready for that yet anyway," she told Rosalie that night over Nepali takeout from a restaurant just up the block. "Moving all my stuff, notifying my clients..."

Rosalie rubbed one hand over Sage's knee beneath the dining table. "Take it slow, babe. We haven't even finished unpacking. Nobody says you have to do everything all at once."

"They *do* have lifts and a grease pit and even a paint booth," Sage salivated.

"You'll get there – when you're ready. In the meantime..." Rosalie turned her attention to the bedroom. "What do you think about getting some plants for that window? Something with a lot of character."

"Like a frizzle sizzle."

"Pardon me?"

Sage laughed. "My nephew learned about them on TV or something and he's been obsessed with them. They look kinda like potted curly fries."

"Yes, exactly like that, then," Rosalie said. "Although I will warn you, I've never actually kept a plant alive. This place needs something, though – it's actually too big for the two of us."

"We'll work on it," Sage promised. "You know, houseplants are starters for fish, which are starters for birds, which are starters for cats... in a mere, oh, thirty years or so, we'll be ready to keep a kid alive."

"Are we sure we've graduated from the pet rock phase?"

"I don't know, do you have one?"

Rosalie snapped her fingers. "Damn, I left it in the condemned building."

Sage shook her head. "Bad rock parent."

"That reminds me... wanna see a crazy video?"

41

Rosalie got out her phone and Sage scooted closer to her. "I found out the city was going to demo my old building so I asked my boss if he wanted me to cover it. He just scoffed and asked who would want to see an apartment building from the fifties get knocked down, so the newspaper didn't cover it. Luckily, somebody recorded it on their phone and uploaded it to YouTube because look what happened."

She hit play and the familiar building appeared on screen, a half-dozen demolition crewmembers standing around in the parking lot. The vantage seemed to be from across the street, and it was lucky for whoever was filming that they weren't any closer.

"I'll skip to the good part," Rosalie said, scrolling forward then stopping as a a crane with a wrecking ball drove into frame.

It took a few swings at the building, punching a few holes in the side of it, and surprisingly quickly, walls started crumbling on their own. The whole building folded in on itself like a book closing, and a massive plume of dust and debris consumed it all.

"Is it supposed to fall down that fast?" Sage asked.

"Definitely not." Rosalie scrolled forward until it was possible to see through the dust, and what was left wasn't much at all. "The sinkhole opened up *while* they were demoing the building, basically swallowed the whole thing."

"Holy shit."

"The crew's okay, made their day a lot shorter than they were expecting," she said. "My boss spent the afternoon stomping around the office, trying to pretend he wasn't mad at himself for telling me not to cover the demo."

"Babe... you could have been *in there*." Sage threw her arms around Rosalie, holding her tight. "Not just as a reporter doing a story, as a resident. What if they didn't inspect the building when they did?"

The thought had occurred to her, and she'd chosen not to dwell on it.

"But they did and no one was hurt," she said. Sage had her cheek pressed to Rosalie's chest so she kissed the top of her head. Then she laughed. "Hey, maybe there'll be a class-action and I'll get a settlement for having lived in a death trap."

"Let's not talk about the death trap anymore."

"Deal. Wanna go to the nursery and pick out a baby plant?"

8

SAGE

They did end up getting a frizzle sizzle, and one for Sage's nephew Robbie too. They'd agonized over name choices and fun pot designs, and against all odds, they'd kept Ms. Frizzle alive.

In the last six months, they'd filled their apartment with all sorts of eclectic and unique décor. Every dish they owned came from a thrift store, chosen on the basis of individual beauty rather than its ability to match with the rest of the set.

Sage reserved time at a glassblowing hot shop downtown a few times a month, a hobby she'd picked up after she finished her training as a mechanic, and she occasionally brought home vases and glassware. Sage always saw the imperfections in the things she made, but Rosalie thought they were beautiful and kept the vases filled with fresh flowers through the summer.

The most notable addition they'd made in their first six months together, once they were sure they could keep a houseplant alive, was a white and tan beagle mix named Bear. They'd adopted him from a shelter and he was Rosalie's first dog, so she spoiled him rotten – which of course undid every effort Sage made to train him.

"He's six, he's stuck in his ways," Rosalie would say whenever Bear tried to steal food off the table or conveniently forgot what 'stay' meant.

"You know that 'can't teach an old dog new tricks' thing is bullshit, right?" Sage would invariably remind her.

"Yeah, but what about a dog who's simply too cute to discipline?"

Bear followed Rosalie around like her shadow, and Sage couldn't blame him – she did the same whenever the opportunity arose.

She loved the way their apartment was a perfect mix of the two of them, blending into one life. She loved how their little family was growing already. But what she loved most was the way her heart never failed to skip a beat when she heard Rosalie's key in the lock.

You'd think after six months, she would have gotten used to the domestic life, would have stopped celebrating each individual homecoming. But when it came to Rosalie, the excitement never died – never even diminished.

Sage had a newfound appreciation for how excited dogs get when their human comes home, because the first thing she wanted to do whenever Rosalie stepped through that door was jump all over her and lick her face.

Tonight, though, she was more excited than ever.

It took every ounce of her willpower to remain in the living room when she heard Rosalie opening the door, home from work. Sage had planned all this out, down to the visual she wanted Rosalie to have when she walked in, and that meant staying put while Bear trotted over to greet their woman.

"Babe?" Rosalie called. Sage heard her dropping her keys on the counter. "I have good news."

"Me too, come in here."

Instead, she heard Rosalie greeting Bear, the jingle of his dog tags, and then the refrigerator door opening. Sage nibbled her lower lip, willing herself not to spoil the surprise.

"My boss is giving me a weekly column," Rosalie called. "Said I can write about whatever I want as long as it applies to the local community."

"That's great," Sage said, shifting from foot to foot.

"He says people like my articles and my writing style, so–"

Finally, she stepped into the doorway, Bear at her heels, and saw Sage standing there in a pair of dress slacks and a button-up shirt, her hair slicked back, the room dimmed by a cluster of taper candles on their dining table, a long-stem rose made of glass in her hand.

Rosalie's eyes went wide and she dropped the cheese stick she'd been eating. Bear didn't miss a beat in cleaning it up for her.

"What are you doing?"

"I have news too," Sage said. "And a question for you."

"Would that question be... a romantic one?"

Sage glanced at the candles flickering behind her and chuckled. "What gave you that impression?"

"Is it... what I think it is?"

Rosalie suddenly looked pale, and alarm shot through Sage's chest. "Would that be bad?"

"No," Rosalie said quickly. "Not at all, I assumed we were moving in that direction. It's fast though, isn't it?"

"I can wait–"

"No," Rosalie repeated, stepping forward and taking one of Sage's hands in her own. "Fast doesn't have to be bad, right? We moved in fast, and that's been good for us."

"It's been wonderful." Sage squeezed Rosalie's hand. "You're kind of cutting to the chase, and I had this whole speech planned out..."

"I'm sorry. Go ahead."

"Well, I was going to tell you my news first, but now that you're expecting it, I guess I better just ask... Rosalie, will you marry me?" She held out the glass rose, turning it so Rosalie could see that one of its leaves had been fashioned into a hook and it held a sparkling gold engagement ring, unique just like Rosalie.

"Did you make this?" Rosalie asked, admiring the rose instead of the ring.

"I wanted to give you flowers when I proposed, but I didn't want them to die," she explained. "Now you'll have something to remember this moment by... if it's a yes?"

Rosalie grinned, then she looked down at Bear. "What do you think? Should I keep her?"

He watched her with keen interest, waiting to see what she'd do... and whether she would drop any more cheese on the floor.

Rosalie turned back to Sage. "I think he votes yes." She stepped into Sage's arms, her hands grabbing hungrily at her hips. "I do too. I would love nothing more than to be your wife."

Sage plucked the ring off the hooked leaf. "I picked something out of the ordinary because you're no ordinary woman. This is hematite – the same color as your eyes."

The ring had a large, dark gray central stone, with a circle of small diamonds around it. As she slipped it on Rosalie's finger, it caught the light from the candles and did exactly what she'd expected – it made her eyes pop beautifully.

"I love it, and I love you." Rosalie laid a deep, impassioned kiss on her. And then Sage felt Bear headbutting her leg.

"And we love you too."

Then the doorbell rang and Sage explained, "I ordered takeout from the fancy Italian place you like. I wanted you to have your favorite food tonight, but I also wanted to have you all to myself."

They were halfway through an exquisite meal of mushroom carbonara and wedding daydreams when Rosalie sat up tall and kicked Sage under the table.

"Ouch! What was that for?"

"You never told me your news!"

"Oh shit, I forgot." Sage chuckled. "It's the whole reason I proposed tonight, actually. Henry has an open stall in his garage and I'm gonna take it."

"That's awesome, honey, I'm excited for you." Rosalie got out of her chair to hug Sage, and Bear took the opportunity to try to steal a noodle.

"Down," Sage snapped her fingers, then scooped Rosalie onto her lap. "I'll be able to do more extensive repairs with access to all that professional equipment, so we'll be able to afford the wedding you deserve."

"All I want is one that includes you."

9

ROSALIE

THE PRESENT

All I want is a wedding that includes you.

That was what Rosalie said six months ago, before wedding planning turned her loved ones into crab cake throwing monsters.

How had they gotten here? On a road paved with good intentions – a compromise here to satisfy Sage's mother, a capitulation there to keep the wedding party happy. Rosalie hadn't been the kind of girl who fantasized about her wedding when she was young. Hell, she hadn't figured out until after college that the reason she never had any dreams of 'Mr. Right' was because she wasn't looking for a *mister* at all.

Sage's dream wedding was a similarly blank canvas, but for different reasons. She said one night while they were poring over Pinterest boards full of reception décor that she'd never bothered to come up with one because she never saw herself getting married.

"You still can't convince me I'm good enough for

you," she'd added, and Rosalie pulled her into a playful headlock.

"Stop saying that, you're amazing."

When they got engaged, neither of them really knew what to expect, what they wanted, or how to plan a wedding. They just knew they wanted each other.

Six months into planning, the big day was getting closer every day – it was two months away – and Rosalie still didn't feel like she really had a handle on the planning process. She certainly didn't know how to handle Sage's mom, who was the sweetest woman but the definition of a helicopter parent... or even her own relatives at this point.

Last week, Rosalie had opened her email to find that the wedding planner, Stella, had sent her a guest list *for the menu tasting*.

"That seems excessive," she said, showing the list to Sage. "Isn't it usually just the engaged couple that goes to that?"

Sage shrugged. "My mom said she'd like to come so she can account for various distant relatives' food allergies. That seemed reasonable because I can't remember them all. Everybody else on that list? I have no clue."

Rosalie had called Stella to ask, "Isn't the venue coordinator going to be pissed if she has to feed a dozen people?"

"No, not at all, you're paying good money to have your wedding at this location," she'd reassured her. "You deserve to have the food you want... besides, you're far from the most demanding brides they'll work with this season."

"I'm not the demanding one," Rosalie had grumbled under her breath as she hung up.

So today, the entire wedding party had showed up to decide on the menu. And from the very first resentful look the venue owner shot in Rosalie and Sage's direction, they knew this was *not* typical.

"The building is beautiful, look at that original woodwork," Stella was marveling as the group made their way toward the long rectangular table that had been set up for them at one end of the ballroom. "Can I see your portfolio again, remind myself what it looks like all filled up?"

The owner, Sue, spoke through her teeth, "I can track that down for you when I get a minute." The implication being that Stella was asking too much – an opinion Rosalie happened to share.

Sue redirected everyone's attention to the table. "Please have a seat. I'm sorry it's a little echo-y in here without a crowd. Ordinarily we host tastings in our conference room. It's too small for this group, though."

"Thank you so much for accommodating all of us," Sage said as her parents, her sister and her kids, Rosalie's dad, and Casey all found seats around the table. Rosalie did a little steering, pointing her dad to a seat that faced away from the bar, then headed toward Sage at the other end of the table.

"I'll tell our chef we're ready to begin," Sue said, marching off toward the kitchen.

"I can't believe we're doing the tasting at last," Stella

said, beating Rosalie to the chair at the head of the table that she'd been aiming for. "I thought we'd never get here."

"Never? My head's spinning with how fast this wedding is coming together," Sage's dad said.

"Robbie, move over next to me," Sage's sister, Willow, said to her four-year-old son.

"But I wanna sit next to Aunt Sage," he pouted.

"Well, I'm sure Aunt Rosalie does too." Willow patted the empty chair next to her and the little boy grudgingly moved down, opening up a chair on the other side of Sage.

"Thank you, Robbie," Rosalie said. Willow and her kids – the ones old enough to talk – had been referring to her as Aunt Rosalie ever since the proposal, and hearing it never failed to make her chest bloom with warmth.

"You know this wasn't an invitation to get a free meal, right, sis?" Sage said with a wry glance toward the kids.

Willow stuck her tongue out, then gestured to the baby nestled into a wrap against her chest. "What am I supposed to do with three kids below school age while I'm traipsing all around town for your wedding?"

"What traipsing are you doing?"

"The dress fitting, all those damn jelly bean wedding favors I helped you two stuff into bags last weekend, this..."

Sage made a *yap, yap, yap* gesture with one hand. "Yeah, yeah, I did all that and more for your wedding so you owe me."

Rosalie cued in to the other people around the table.

Her dad was keeping to himself, looking out of place and mildly uncomfortable.

Casey was ignoring him – not his biggest fan – but she was being a good sport listening to Stella explain how the reason they were having a food tasting so late in the game was because this was actually their second-choice venue, and the first one had fallen through. Double-booked, a nightmare-inducing situation that Rosalie immediately tuned back out of lest she relive that particular trauma.

And two seats down, Rosalie could just make out Sage's mom, Angela, talking quietly to Sage's dad, Scott. "I just don't see what the rush is. First she moves out and now she's getting married... what's next, are they going to move away from us?"

She should stop listening. It was obviously not a conversation that was meant to be shared. But every time Rosalie spent time with Sage's parents, she came away with the impression that Angela in particular was holding her at arm's length.

"She does not hate you," Sage had reassured her on a host of different occasions. "She's just, you know, the typical reserved midwestern white lady."

"So you're saying she acts the same with Willow's husband?"

"Um, yes," Sage had answered, not at all convincingly.

Now, Rosalie might finally get a little insight into what it was about herself that Angela didn't like, so she listened harder when she knew she shouldn't.

"Lots of people get married before they've been together a year," Scott pointed out. "We barely made it past that milestone ourselves."

"Well, we had a particular imperative to make it quick," Angela said with a nervous chuckle.

"And that's a better reason to be married?"

"I just don't want her to make a mistake."

That was the invisible punch to the gut that Rosalie deserved for listening in on a conversation she had no business hearing. Still hurt, though, and left her puzzling over whole new questions. What about marrying her would be a mistake?

"How are we doing, folks?" Sue asked as she reappeared with a couple of wait staff flanking her. "I've got several cocktail hour options for you to try – prosciutto-wrapped figs, shrimp cocktail skewers, pigs in a blanket, crab cakes and mini spinach quiches."

Everyone settled down and stuffed their faces for a couple minutes, and then Sue asked hopefully, "Well, what's the consensus?"

There was none.

Between nine adults and three children, everyone seemed to have a strong opinion about something, and no one was willing to compromise.

"And this is just the appetizer," Sage said against Rosalie's temple. "Kill me now."

"We should just slip out the back door and let them fight amongst themselves," Rosalie suggested, only half joking.

After more than ten minutes of discussion that

quickly devolved into bickering, Sage stood up and announced, "We'd like shrimp cocktail skewers and pigs in a blanket. Next dish, please."

"Coming right up," Sue said, her brow glistening when she turned back toward the kitchen.

Sage's butt had no sooner touched her chair again than half the group was contesting her decision.

"What about Aunt Aggie, who doesn't eat meat?" her mom asked loudly. "Isn't that why I'm here?"

"Aunt Aggie's not the only one who's going to be at the wedding," Sage said. "And we would have more hors d'oeuvre if we could afford it, but we can't."

"Maybe you shouldn't have picked such a fancy venue, then," Rosalie's dad said, and she sent him a shocked glare. Since when did he care? He'd been happy not to get involved with the wedding planning when she decided to spare him the stress, and she hadn't asked him to pay for any of it.

"We took what was still available when our first venue cancelled," she reminded him.

"Miraculously available," Stella chimed in. "This place is beautiful – we got lucky."

The appetizer and salad course tastings went pretty much the same way. Nobody could agree on anything and everyone had a Very Compelling Reason why their opinion was the most important. Every time Sage or Rosalie made an executive decision, it made someone unhappy, and Rosalie could see the annoyance in Sue's eyes. Every time she came out of the kitchen with a new course, they screamed *this is why you don't invite your whole damn family to a menu tasting.*

No shit, Sue, Rosalie thought.

"I need a drink," she said, turning to Sage. "Can I get you one?"

"I'm not sure the bar is open."

"At this point, they already think our families are a bunch of animals," Rosalie said under her breath. "What could one more indiscretion hurt?"

She went over to the long mahogany bar tucked into the corner of the event hall, slipping behind it and helping herself to a bottle of vodka and a cocktail glass. Sue could add it to their tab, which was already astronomically higher than Rosalie had anticipated.

She didn't need the drink nearly as much as she needed a little distance from that table full of chaos and she lingered behind the bar, watching her dad sip on a glass of ice water. He'd been doing well lately – at least as far as she knew. But there was a lot of booze at weddings. Could he handle the temptation? Was it even fair to ask him to?

"My god, it's hairy out there." Casey stepped behind the bar and slung an arm around Rosalie's shoulder. "You okay?"

"Yeah, I just needed a breather," she said.

Casey got a glass and mixed herself a rum and Coke. "Cheers."

They drank, and Rosalie grimaced slightly. Casey laughed, looking at the bottle Rosalie had selected.

CARA MALONE

"If you're gonna help yourself, you could at least pick something off the top shelf."

"Not my area of expertise."

They watched Willow's toddler daughter, Katie, stand up on her chair. She and Willow were arguing about something, and then Katie lifted the front of her dress, announcing, "I'm not a baby. I'm wearing big girl panties, see?"

Willow yanked Katie back into her seat, then covered her face with her hands.

"You sure you're ready to marry into that family?" Casey snorted under her breath.

"Katie's only... two and a half, I think? She doesn't know any better."

"Yeah, but then there's everyone else."

"Well, my family's no prize either," Rosalie sighed as she looked at her dad. Who knew where her mom was, or what she was like these days? She'd left before Rosalie even started school. And her extended family lived out of town – that was the only thing that kept them from being just as overbearing as Angela.

"At least you have me," Casey said with a cheeky smile. "I'm awesome."

"You are," Rosalie agreed. "Thanks for coming to check on me."

She spotted Sue coming back with the entrees and they returned to the table.

"Everything okay?" Sage whispered.

Rosalie kissed her temple. "Perfect, babe. Ooh, the strip steak looks good."

The first crab cake was flung just a few minutes later, right when Rosalie thought they were nearing the end of this ordeal. Katie stood up on her chair again and Rosalie's dad suggested – only semi-joking – that she be strapped down.

"But I'm a big girl," Katie objected.

"She's fine," Willow added, tugging on her daughter's arm with one hand and cutting a piece of steak for Robbie with the other.

"She's feral," Rosalie's dad grumbled under her breath, and Willow abruptly stood.

"Excuse me?"

Rosalie's pulse pounded in her ears and she scrambled for an excuse she could make for her dad. What the hell was he thinking? Before she could smooth things over, food was flying around the table and Sage was grabbing her hand, pulling her to safety behind the bar.

The food fight only lasted a minute or two, but that was enough time to nail the wallpaper, each other, and even one of the chandeliers. Sue came running out of the kitchen yelling, "What is wrong with you people?!" and neither Rosalie nor Sage could muster a defense.

The whole party got kicked out of the building, and on the steps, Sue informed them that they could look for another venue for the wedding because she wasn't risking another incident like that in her ballroom.

"But there are less than two months until the wedding!" Stella objected, near tears.

"Maybe the *zoo* will take you – you certainly belong

there," Sue said, then slammed the door shut and locked it.

"I want to help her clean up," Sage said. "Should I knock?"

Rosalie sighed. "Let's just go."

"I really don't know where we're going to find a venue big enough for the crowd we're expecting on such short notice," Stella worried on the way to the parking lot.

"You could have it in my back yard," Angela offered.

Rosalie's dad snorted, "Oh, you'd love that, wouldn't you?"

"What's that supposed to mean?" Angela scowled at him.

"Stop it! All of you!" Rosalie shouted, and there was silence for the very first time since they arrived.

She stomped off toward her car, and Sage chased after her. Rosalie got in and put her finger on the ignition button, but paused.

"What's wrong?" Sage asked. "You know, besides... everything?"

"I can't even trust my loved ones not to say awful things or throw food at each other. How did we get here?"

"We took the highway, but we can go the back roads home if you want..."

Sage was looking at her with those puppy dog eyes that never failed to warm her heart, no matter how bad her day was going. Rosalie chuckled.

"Thank you... but you know what I mean."

Sage sat back in her seat, pensive. "It's taken our whole lives, a million or more tiny decisions and nudges from the universe, to get to this point. Some of them have been wonderful, some were undoubtedly mistakes – like allowing Stella to invite the entire wedding party to our menu tasting. But they can't *really* be mistakes, because they led me to you."

Rosalie punched her shoulder. "Cheeseball."

"Ooh, that could be a good appetizer, you know, for when the wedding ends up in my parents' back yard."

10

SAGE

TEN YEARS AGO

S age stood outside, feeling the breeze on her skin and
the sun baking down on her hair for the first time in
close to a month.

On one hand, it was a relief to feel normal again, to
feel free, to enjoy something as simple as the weather.

On the other, her entire life had just changed in the
course of twenty-six days and it would never truly be
normal again, so what business did the sun have to shine
or the birds to chirp when everything in Sage's world was
so upside down? It wasn't fair, things just going on like
they always had, like nothing had changed.

"Here comes Mom."

Sage flinched. She'd almost forgotten that her dad
was standing beside her, and he frowned.

"Still feeling hazy from the meds?" he asked.

"The doctor said it'll take a while to get used to
them."

Or they wouldn't work right and she'd have to try a

whole new cocktail of drugs. Or they would all make her feel like her thoughts were traveling through mud and she'd be hazy from now on. Or she'd forget to take them, the delusions and hallucinations would bubble back up and she'd end up back in the hospital again. There were a whole bunch of delightful possibilities to choose from now.

Her mom's car pulled up to the curb and her dad helped her into the back seat as if she was weak and helpless.

"I can handle it," she said, batting his hand away.

"I'm just trying to help."

"Well, stop."

Her mother was frowning too when Sage looked at her. There had been a lot of frowning in the past few weeks, some crying, a little bit of wall punching – that last had been Sage's reaction when she learned she'd be going to live with her parents for a while instead of back to her apartment.

She buckled her seatbelt and crossed her arms over her chest. Basically, doubling down on the shitty attitude rather than just apologizing for being snippy with her dad, who totally meant well, because what else is a nineteen-year-old to do in that situation?

"We should stop at the pharmacy on the way home if you're up for it," her mom said once everyone was in the car.

"Yeah, that's fine."

"Or I could drop you off first."

"I said it's fine."

"Well, I wasn't sure if you were tired–"

"*Mom.* I'm not made of glass all of a sudden, okay?"

They sat in silence until the person in line behind them honked and the hospital valet started waving them along. "I'm sorry. This is all just new to me," Sage's mom said, then put the car in drive.

They got all the way to the highway before Sage made herself say, "I'm sorry too."

They arrived home about an hour later with a pharmacy bag full of rattling pill bottles, a fresh notebook because Sage's new psychiatrist had recommended keeping a journal, and a takeout bag of hot, greasy burgers and fries because the psych ward's food was shit and Sage had come out of there ten pounds lighter than when she went in.

"I am tired after all," she fibbed as her dad started portioning the food out on plates at the dining table. "Mind if I eat in my room?"

"Whatever you need, sweetie," her mom said. "Can I have a hug?"

She asked tentatively, like she wasn't sure whether Sage would go all praying mantis on her and bite her head off, and guilt surged in her throat. She went to her mother and let her wrap her arms around her, breathing in the comforting scent of bergamot that had always felt like safety to her. She waved her hand at her father. "Dad, get in here."

Three weeks ago, it would have been an entirely too-long hug, but right now, it felt nice. Consoling, if not curative.

Sage was the first to break away. She took her burger, fries, and bag full of meds down the hall to her childhood bedroom. She tossed the pharmacy bag on her dresser and set her lunch on the bed, but instead of eating, she just lay back, propped up on a couple pillows, looking around the room.

It was exactly as she left it when she moved out a year and a half ago. There were fresh cotton sheets on the bed instead of the flannel ones she was using back then, and her mom had obviously dusted and vacuumed in here because everything was clean. It was a decent-size room with an attached bathroom, but it shared a wall with her parents' bedroom and it was not where Sage had pictured herself at this point in her life.

She had a place of her own, with roommates. A mildly crappy job doing oil changes. She was halfway through an automotive service tech program at a technical college, and she was flirting with a cute redhead enrolled in the cosmetology program at her school.

Well, not anymore.

Now she lived with her parents and took antipsychotic drugs and had to train herself not to listen to the *very fucking realistic voices* that had begun talking over her shoulder.

She sat up and stuffed a fry in her mouth.

Damn it. It was so much better than hospital food.

11

ROSALIE

NINE YEARS AGO

R osalie was ugly crying in her dorm room when her phone chimed.

She almost didn't check it. Her phone was the whole reason she was sitting here with hot cheeks and puffy red eyes and a tear-stained dress...

Oh shit.

The dress brought her back to the present and she flipped over her phone after all. Sure enough, there was a text from her date tonight, who she'd completely forgotten about after she got a call from her aunt.

I'm here, the text read.

Rosalie got up and assessed the damage in the mirror hanging on the back of the door. Her eye makeup was all smeared and she'd cried so much there was an actual puddle of tears on her dress – which just so happened to fall right at her crotch, making it look like she'd not only gone on a crying jag but also pissed herself.

Perfect for a first date.

She really should just call Adam and tell him the date was off. She could feign illness, and with all that crying swelling her throat, she'd probably be convincing.

But then her aunt would win, and by extension, so would her dad.

Aunt Kathy wanted Rosalie to come home and dedicate herself to taking care of her father, setting aside all her own hopes, ambitions and desires. She wanted Rosalie to sacrifice her own future for her father's present.

The word *selfish* had come up more than once during their conversation, and Aunt Kathy wasn't entirely off-base. Aunt Kathy lived on the other side of the country and Rosalie was all her dad had. She knew he wasn't doing well all by himself back home. She knew he'd be doing better if she was there.

But for how long?

How long until they destroyed each other?

That was why she came to New York for college, but it was also why she'd spent the last half-hour sobbing into her date-night dress.

"Aunt Kathy doesn't know the whole story," she reminded herself as she picked up her phone and told Adam she'd be down in five minutes.

He sent back a quick reply. Well, letter, really. Just *K*. Not much of a talker, apparently, at least over text. He sat in front of Rosalie and Casey in their freshman English class and Casey kept saying how cute he was.

"I'd like to lick his abs," to be more precise, so Rosalie felt guilty when Adam asked her out instead of Casey.

But her bestie insisted she accept, and so here she was.

She stripped off the tear-stained dress and tossed another, plainer one over her head. She grabbed her purse, snatched one of Casey's travel makeup remover cloths, then dashed down the hall to the girls' bathroom to scrub the smeared mascara off her cheeks. No time to reapply, she was going natural tonight.

When she found Adam waiting outside the dorm, he was gracious about having to wait.

"I just got a little behind schedule," she said as he took her hand without asking and started to lead her toward the subway at the edge of campus.

"I do that all the time, it's no problem."

Adam turned out to be *slightly* chattier in person than he was in texts, and by the time they got to the subway, Rosalie knew he was from Virginia and he was a pre-med student. It was shaping up to be a pretty run-of-the-mill date, and she'd even managed to put Aunt Kathy out of her head for the time being.

And then they got to the yellowish light of the subway platform, Adam got a look at her for the first time and said, "Holy shit, did somebody punch you in the face?"

"What?"

"Your eyes are all swollen. What happened?"

Rosalie looked around, trying to find a reflective surface to assess the situation. She'd been rushing when she washed her makeup off, but it couldn't be that bad, could it? Frustration started to well up in her chest. Did this night have to be a complete and utter shitshow?

"I was crying earlier," she admitted. She really would have liked to keep that to herself, especially when it came to a guy she only knew four things about. *Adam. Virginia. Pre-med. Casey wants to do disgusting things with his abs.*

He put his hands on her face and she flinched away, then steadied herself. "This looks like more than just crying. Does it hurt?"

"No–" Rosalie brought a hand to her eyelid and winced as her skin screamed at the contact.

"I think you're having an allergic reaction or something," Adam said.

"Shit." Casey's stupid makeup remover wipe, this was why Rosalie never borrowed her stuff – they were complete opposites when it came to skin type. Casey could scrub her face with a Brillo pad and she'd be glowing. "It really hurts."

The train had arrived and people were pouring out of it. The looks they were giving Rosalie were far from reassuring and she used a window on one of the train cars to inspect her face. Sure enough, everywhere the makeup wipe had touched was now raw, red and angry.

"We should go to the hospital," Adam said.

Rosalie snorted. "Yeah, right. I can't afford that."

"Then at least the student health center. They can give you something to make it feel better."

"I'm fine." She was broke, and the health center was cheaper than the hospital but it wasn't free.

"Come on, I insist."

69

Adam took her hand again, turning her around and guiding her up the subway steps. They walked back across campus to the twenty-four-hour health center near the student union and got a soothing ointment for Rosalie's face, and when it was time to settle the bill, Adam whipped out his wallet.

"I'll pay for it," Rosalie said.

"A woman does not pay for anything on a date," he answered, shoving his credit card at the nurse practitioner while Rosalie suppressed the urge to roll her eyes. On the one hand, barf. On the other, not having to pay for this stupid cream she didn't want in the first place meant she wouldn't have to cancel pizza night with Casey next week.

So Adam bought her the damn ointment – it really did help – and then they went next door and he bought her a Frappuccino and a muffin from the coffee cart in the student union before she begged off on the rest of the date.

When they got back to her dorm, he asked if they could go out again, and Rosalie looked at him like he was crazy. "After *that*, really?"

He just shrugged. "I've had worse first dates."

"So have I," Rosalie admitted.

"Besides, this one wasn't a fair trial. It's not like any of that was on purpose."

So Rosalie agreed to a second date, even though she already knew there was no spark between them. There never was, and she was starting to think there was something wrong with her. Adam was a nice guy at least, more than she could say for some of the creeps she'd gone out with who'd gotten handsy in the first five minutes.

She went inside and took a detour to the bathroom to reapply the ointment. Her eyelids were now shiny in addition to being puffy and raw, and if it didn't get better by Monday, she was going to look *awesome* for the interview had scheduled with the university president for the school paper.

There was a light on under the door when she got back to her room, and she found Casey listening to music on her bed, flipping through biology flashcards.

"Are you back already?" she asked, sitting up and catching sight of Rosalie's face. "Holy shit, did Adam do that to you?"

She was off the bed in an instant, cradling Rosalie's face in her hands, rage in her eyes.

"I'll kill him."

"Relax, it wasn't Adam. He was actually pretty sweet."

"What happened?"

"I got in a fight with my aunt."

Casey frowned. "The one who lives in Montana?"

"Yeah, long story." And because she now had nothing better to do with her evening, Rosalie told it to her – every ugly detail, right down to the awful things Aunt Kathy said to her over the phone. "I know damn well I have sensitive skin and normally I wouldn't come within ten feet of some random product I haven't tried before without testing it first." She huffed a sigh. "I think my subconscious was doling out some punishment."

"Punishment? Come on, Rose, you do not deserve to beat yourself up – literally – about going away to college." She and Casey had had this conversation at least a dozen times already, and Rosalie never actually believed her. "Something like seventy percent of the kids here are from out of state."

"Yeah, but they didn't spend the last two years of high school taking care of their single parent. I just left him, Case."

"You chose to do what was best for yourself. That situation was not healthy and he was gonna drag you down with him," Casey said, throwing her arms around Rosalie. "Prioritizing your own needs is not the same thing as being selfish."

"You say that when it's *my* dad," she mumbled against Casey's shoulder. "What if it was yours?"

"Then you'd be giving me the same talk I'm giving you." Casey pulled Rosalie back to look her in the eyes. "Now, the real question, since you're home early... pizza night?"

"With everything."

"On your half. And then you're gonna tell me all about the part of the date that you *did* go on, and how hot Adam looked, and when you're going out with him next. I can't believe he took care of you. What a sweetheart."

"You really should be going on dates with him. He's wasted on me."

Casey just shook her head. "I don't get you, West."

Rosalie laughed. "Me neither."

1 2

SAGE

TWO YEARS AGO

I t was a frigid-cold night with about a foot of snow on the ground. With Willow, her husband Rob, their two-year-old and the new baby all here for dinner, it felt like the small house was bursting at the seams and Sage kept finding excuses to step away, have a breather.

"It's perfectly okay to set boundaries and ask people to accommodate your needs," her therapist's voice echoed in her head.

How many times had she heard that over the last eight years? And yet she always kinda felt like an asshole when she was ignoring people.

"You're not ignoring them, you're taking a moment to yourself," Dr. Khan rebutted in her mind. Who needed auditory hallucinations when your therapist's often-repeated advice was so readily available?

The fact of the matter was Sage loved her sister, absolutely adored her nephew Robbie, and the baby, Katie, was the cutest little chubby-cheeked marshmallow... but they were all loud and the kids never stopped moving and crying and *needing,* and Willow's husband Big Rob was kind of a chatterbox, and their mother hadn't stopped baby-talking at Katie since she got here. Sage's head was spinning and it felt a whole lot better when she was in her quiet bedroom with the door closed.

She'd been living here ever since that first psych ward stay. Her bedroom was a lot more current-Sage and less high-school-Sage, and her dad had let her take over the garage with all her mechanic's tools after she graduated from her program. That was the biggest reason she hadn't moved out – she'd built her business around this house.

But also, somewhere in the back of her mind, she'd started thinking of it as a safe space. A soft landing. A crutch, really, but at home, her mom made sure she never forgot to take her meds. No one ever made her feel weird or different or dangerous because of her diagnosis here. She got to take things at her own pace.

It had taken her almost a year after her diagnosis to get her meds right – Dr. Khan had said that was to be expected.

She took an extra year and a half to complete her automotive tech program, since that first year on the meds was such a shitshow. It was double the time most people did it in, but she got her certification and she started taking clients in her dad's garage.

The redhead from cosmetology was long gone when Sage finally got back to class, of course. She thought about looking her up, maybe being slick and making an appointment at whatever salon she was working in... but the thought of telling her why she'd disappeared stopped Sage cold.

It stopped her from dating for a long while, actually, and she lost touch with a lot of her friends, too. She mostly had Willow for a social life now, and the kids.

In the last eight years, Sage had suffered her share of losses and setbacks. She also had plenty to celebrate, including the therapist who had pulled her out of her initial funk and showed her the good things she still had in her life. Her support systems, her passions.

Sometimes she just needed to catch her breath, and she was working on being okay with that.

She went back downstairs, where Big Rob had cornered her dad and was telling him all about the kitchen renovations he had planned. Robbie was standing with his nose smushed against the glass sliding door to the back yard, begging, "Outside, sled, sled, sled!"

"It's too cold out there, baby," Willow told him. "Besides, you need a hill to sled on."

"I sled," Robbie objected.

Sage went over and scooped him into her arms. He protested when he realized she wasn't going to take him outside, but forgot all about sled riding when his grandma came from the kitchen with warm bread pudding for dessert.

"Cake!" Robbie switched gears, trying to climb over the dining table to get at it.

"Not cake, bread pudding," Sage said, holding him back. She laughed and looked at her sister. "I hope Katie is calmer than this one, for your sake."

"I haven't slept in almost three years," Willow said, reaching for a dessert plate just as Katie woke from the nap she was taking against Willow's chest and started to whine.

"Come to Grammy, baby," their mom said, practically stealing Katie from her swaddle.

Everyone settled into their dessert, and Sage's dad came around with a carafe of coffee, filling mugs. It was as peaceful as they'd been all night – sugar tended to have that effect on the Evans family – and Sage said, "So, I picked up a new hobby."

"Oh yeah?" Big Rob said.

"It suits her perfectly," Sage's mom said. "Never would have thought of it in a million years myself, but it's so Sage."

"Competitive air guitar," Willow guessed.

"Sled!" Robbie chimed in.

"Glassblowing," Sage said, saving them from further guesses.

"I have to show you the paperweight she made," their mom said, hopping up from the table. "It's really pretty!"

"It's kind of muddy and misshapen," Sage apologized, already embarrassed before her mom even produced her first project for inspection. She should have left it at the hot shop.

"It's beautiful," her mom crowed, placing the lump of glass in the center of the table like a precious piece of art. There were little swirls of green and blue inside the clear glass, in no discernible pattern, but it was heavy and flat on one side, so it did technically serve its purpose.

"That's pretty cool, big sis," Willow said, picking it up. "How'd you get into this?"

"Dr. Khan suggested it," Sage said. "Well, she suggested a hobby, and one of the guys I go to group with does glasswork. He's always talking about his latest projects, and he's *way* better than me, but he offered to show me the ropes. I really like it."

The smile on her face was enormous, and for the moment, she wasn't worrying about the sensory overload that had been plaguing her since her sister's family arrived. So, score another point for the good doctor.

"Isn't it dangerous?" Big Rob asked. "All those high temperatures?"

"Well, I wouldn't bring Robbie and Katie to the hot shop with me," Sage said.

"And she did come home with a pretty nasty burn on her wrist a couple weeks ago," her dad added.

"Hazard of the trade," Sage shrugged, remembering the exquisite pain that had come with her carelessness when she was shaping the paperweight. "You learn from your mistakes fast or else."

"What do you think, Robbie?" Willow asked, holding the paperweight out to show him.

"Snowball fight," he said, reaching for it.

Sage chuckled. "Not unless you want a concussion, little man."

13

ROSALIE

TWO YEARS AGO

"This is just for a couple of months until I can get an apartment of my own," Rosalie said as her father helped her unload the trunk of her car.

There was a pit in her stomach and it had been there ever since she agreed to move back into her dad's house two weeks ago. Part of her knew that this was a disastrous idea and only bad things would come of it. That part of her had been having recurring nightmares about being trapped in her childhood home, literally – locked doors everywhere she turned, ropes tying her to the fixtures, her feet sinking into quicksand whenever she tried to leave.

She'd almost called this off half a dozen times in the last couple of weeks, but the practical side of her knew it was her only option.

Living in New York City for the better part of a decade had been wonderful and exciting and valuable. Eye-opening too. About a year after she graduated, she *finally* figured out why she never had chemistry with nice, attractive guys like Adam.

A woman Rosalie worked with asked her out on a date, and Rosalie surprised herself by saying yes. The biggest surprise of the night was how right it felt, how everything clicked into place after so many years of wondering what the hell was wrong with her. She went home after that date feeling like a new woman with the whole world opening up to her... and like the biggest cliché ever, after spending half her life looking for love in all the wrong places.

Things hadn't worked out with her coworker – probably for the best – and Rosalie was still looking for Ms. Right, but she was starting to suspect that her future wife didn't live in the Big Apple.

The city was also expensive, and no matter how hard she tried to rise up the ranks at the newspaper, she just kept getting passed over for promotions and she never managed to escape the paycheck-to-paycheck life.

Then six months ago, three things happened in quick succession.

Casey moved home to be closer to her parents after her dad fell off his roof while cleaning his gutters.

The local newspaper in Hickory Harbor had an opening for an experienced reporter, which just so happened to pay twice what Rosalie was making, in a city where the cost of living was less than half as much as New York.

And the big one... her dad reached out to her.

He'd sunk deeper into his alcoholism while she was

in college, getting mean and unpredictable, so Rosalie had distanced herself. They'd lost touch for much of the last eight years, speaking only a handful of times, and Rosalie mostly tried not to think about it. Aunt Kathy never stopped blaming her for abandoning her dad, and when Rosalie dwelled on it too much, she blamed herself too.

But when he reached out, he was different. He'd been going to meetings, he hadn't had a drink for six months, and he seemed to be taking responsibility for his part in the dissolution of their relationship.

"I know now that my drinking had a negative impact on you growing up," he'd said that first time they talked six months ago. "I couldn't see it before – I didn't think I was hurting anyone but myself."

It was the understatement of the century, and it didn't acknowledge anything that had happened in the last eight years, what it was like being a new adult cut off from the parent who had raised her. But it was a start.

And so they talked – mostly in text messages, little snippets that were just toes in the water, neither of them ready to take the plunge until Rosalie told her father about the job opening at the Hickory Harbor Gazette last month.

"Take it," he said immediately. "I'd love to have you closer, that way we can really get to know each other again."

"I don't know if I can afford to move right now," she answered. She was locked into the cycle of using up her paycheck the minute she got it to pay overdue bills, and it was hard to imagine coming up with money to move, to pay the first and last months' rent at a new place.

"Let me help you."

"I don't know..."

"You wouldn't believe how much money you can save when you're not putting away a twelve-pack every night," he continued. "I've been a shitty dad the past few years. Let me make it up to you."

Rosalie barely held back a snort – it was another massive understatement – but she considered his offer for a minute before saying, "I don't want to put that kind of strain on our relationship when we just started talking again."

It took another week of cajoling, during which time Rosalie sent in an application to the Gazette just for kicks. Her dad offered up her old bedroom and her gut reaction was a big old *hell no!* but when she got the job, she started to consider it.

A couple of months at home, saving every paycheck instead of being forced to spend every cent... By her calculations, she could be out of her dad's house in three months, tops.

Plus, she'd be near Casey again.

She'd be a big fish in a small pond instead of a perpetual cub reporter that her editor never seemed to notice.

And maybe she'd even meet some new women, ones who were more like her than the big-city party girls she'd been meeting.

And so here she was, setting down her bags in her

cramped and dusty childhood bedroom against her better judgment. The house smelled musty and neglected, and it was like a cave with all the blinds closed. Just as isolating and depressing as she remembered it.

Maybe now that her dad wasn't drinking anymore, he wouldn't feel so inclined to make his surroundings so cave-like and she could make the house feel more lived in.

One step at a time, though.

She came into the living room and asked, "Should we get takeout for dinner? Catch up?"

"That sounds nice." Her dad frowned. "But I sort of figured you would want to get settled in tonight, so I made plans to stay out of your hair. I'm going over to Benny's to watch the game."

"Benny." Rosalie narrowed her eyes. Benny was her dad's best friend from high school, but all Rosalie thought of when she heard his name was the fact that she'd never seen him sober. "Is it... safe... to hang out with him?"

"Safe?"

She shrugged, trying to keep her tone casual. "Aren't you supposed to cut ties with people who enable you when you're in recovery?"

"Benny's my best friend."

That was all her dad had to say on that subject, and he left for Benny's house down the street shortly thereafter. Rosalie tried to keep herself occupied with unpacking her bags, but all she could think about was how quick she'd been to believe her dad – that he was sober, that he'd changed, that he was ready to be her dad.

She didn't *really* know anything about his life now, or how committed he was to doing better. Would he come home from his drinking buddy's house reeking of alcohol? Would he be blatant about it or try to hide it? Was moving back in with him the biggest fucking mistake she'd ever made?

He was sober when he came home that night, but Rosalie never stopped being on edge after that, never stopped waiting for the other shoe to drop.

After three months and six paychecks, she had the bare minimum required to lease the worst apartment in Hickory Harbor. It was still a thousand times better than the worst apartment in New York City, and she was more than tired of walking on eggshells, waiting for her father to turn back into the man she'd known when she was a teenager. So she got a one-year lease and got the hell out of there.

And Aunt Kathy continued to make Rosalie's life more difficult all the way from Montana.

"Your dad just called me, he sounded tearful," she said over the phone the day after Rosalie moved into her new place.

"I talked to him yesterday, he was fine," Rosalie said. She had the phone on speaker and she was working on unpacking the meager possessions that had moved from place to place with her. Casey was going to come over soon, and she was trying to make the apartment as presentable as it could be.

"He's upset you moved out so fast," Aunt Kathy said. "He thinks he drove you away."

He did, Rosalie thought.

"The house is small, and the plan was always for me to stay there just until I could afford the deposit on a place of my own," she told her aunt.

"He liked having you there."

She was gearing up for a long-distance guilt trip. Rosalie had experienced them enough times to know when one was coming, and she'd learned to endure them with a pasted-on smile. She tuned her aunt out while she continued unpacking her small collection of baking tools, and then there was a knock at the door.

"It's open," she called.

"What's that?" Aunt Kathy asked.

"Casey just got here," Rosalie explained. "We're gonna order takeout for dinner."

"You just leave your door unlocked?"

"Hickory Harbor isn't NYC," she reminded her aunt. Casey came in and Rosalie mouthed *Aunt Kathy* to her, pointing at the phone. Casey rolled her eyes.

"Why don't you invite your dad to join you two for dinner?" Kathy suggested. "I'm sure he's sitting home all by himself since you left him."

"Goodbye, Aunt Kathy," Casey said, reaching over and tapping the *End Call* button.

Rosalie's mouth dropped open. "Did you just hang up on my aunt?"

"I don't know why you answered in the first place, she's awful every time she calls."

Rosalie huffed. She couldn't argue the truth of that. "She's my aunt, and she lives far away."

"So?"

"So she needs me to keep an eye on my dad since she can't."

"If she cared that much, she'd drag her ass back from North Dakota or wherever."

"Montana."

"Rose," Casey braced her hands on Rosalie's shoulders, "just because they're family doesn't give them the right to treat you like shit." She looked around the apartment. "Your best friend, on the other hand... You really did take the first place you could find, didn't you?"

Rosalie looked at the small apartment again through Casey's eyes. She'd gotten somewhat used to it already, but now she noticed the cracked plaster walls, the old water stains on the ceiling, the radiator putting off an insufficient amount of heat in the corner of the living room. This was no palace, but at least it wasn't her dad's house.

She was *never* living there again, no matter how guilty it made her feel.

"It's not that bad. I'll give you the tour."

14

SAGE

TWO YEARS AGO

S age had been reserving time at the hot shop once a week for close to a year, graduating from lumpy paperweights to actual usable vessels. She still didn't think her work was good enough to show anyone outside the shop – all of them were beginners at one point too so they understood her struggles. But she was getting better, and she understood why Dr. Khan told her to get a hobby.

It focused her, gave her something to look forward to and work toward every week. It widened her social circle from the basically zero that she'd let it dwindle down to after her diagnosis.

And then there was the unexpected benefit of all the eye candy.

For whatever reason, glassblowing seemed to attract queer artists, and Sage had seen a number of cute girls with impressive arm muscles sweating in front of the glory hole.

"Do you talk to them?" Dr. Khan asked in one of their sessions.

"The cute girls?"

"Yes."

"They don't want to talk to me."

"What makes you think that?" Dr. Khan never accepted anything at face-value. Sage thought it was her most annoying trait, but she did tend to have a point more often than not.

"They're busy," Sage shrugged. "And they probably already have partners."

"Do you only talk to single people?"

Ugh, Dr. Khan. "No," she admitted.

"So why not just say hi next time someone comes into the shop who catches your eye?"

Sage did, if only to report to her therapist that she'd done her homework. That woman's name was Amber and she had a leopard print tattoo over her bare shoulder.

She was friendly, but she got a minor burn that day and she never came back to the hot shop again.

Sage said hi to Dominique, who turned out to be straight, and Melissa, a snob who didn't want to talk to anyone at the hot shop who wasn't a Serious Artist. There were Rachel and Lara, who were cool and fun to hang out with, but they were a couple.

And then one day Lucy came in.

She wasn't intimidated by the hot shop, or straight, or a snob, or taken. She had long blonde hair that she kept back in neat French braids, and she pulled cane like a seasoned professional. Sage admired her from afar for a couple of weeks until the Dr. Khan, Rachel and Lara all conspired to get her to introduce herself.

She said hello.

She stepped in and assisted Lucy with the piece she was working on.

She asked her out to lunch afterward.

All of it was going wonderfully for the first time since she'd started putting herself out there socially again. And maybe she could even try opening up... romantically?

And then at the end of the meal, the server came over and asked, "One check or two?"

"One," Sage said.

"Two," Lucy answered at the same time.

And before they'd even had a chance, Sage knew they weren't on the same page after all.

"I'm sorry, I didn't mean to give you the impression this was a date," Lucy said.

The server looked awkwardly between them, and Sage tried to insist on paying for lunch anyway, though she knew she'd already lost the battle. The server split up the check and the awkwardness persisted as they finished their drinks and headed outside.

Just let it go, she tried to tell herself, but something petulant was building in her chest.

"I should head home – got work in the morning," Lucy said.

"Okay." Sage almost let her walk away, almost succeeded in brushing off the awkwardness of the end of their not-date. But just as Lucy was turning to go, Sage reached out and brushed her arm. "Can I ask you something?"

Lucy turned back, an apologetic look on her face like she already knew where this was going. "I'm sorry, Sage–"

"I just don't get it," she said. "I thought we were having a good time."

"We were. It's just–"

"I don't understand what's not good enough about me," Sage blurted. "I thought..." If whatever turned Lucy off before hadn't sealed her fate, this little outburst of low self-esteem certainly would.

Lucy gave her a pitying look. God, Sage hated those. "It's not that you're not good enough. I like you."

"Just not romantically." They barely knew each other. Lucy hadn't stuck around long enough to learn any of the *legitimate* reasons someone might shy away from dating Sage, and she still wasn't interested.

Lucy shrugged, like this was nothing to her. "You're just not my type. What can I say, I'm into the femme end of the spectrum. Sorry."

And then she headed up the sidewalk, and Sage stood there holding back tears. So now on top of everything else, she wasn't feminine enough. She stomped back to the hot shop, wondering how often she'd have to endure bumping into Lucy there now, and took great satisfaction in smashing her latest piece to bits before adding it back to the molten glass in the glory hole.

15

ROSALIE

A YEAR AND A HALF AGO

"You have a good job and you live in a very affordable city. There's no reason not to upgrade your car."

That was an argument Casey's dad had been making to Rosalie for over a year. On a technical level, he was right. Rosalie had inherited her cherry-red Honda Civic from her grandmother, who'd been one of those stereotypical 'only took it to church once a week' drivers and had willed it to her in excellent condition, even if it was already twenty years old when she got it.

"I barely drove it in New York," Rosalie countered. "And it's got almost no rust on it, which is basically a miracle."

She was having breakfast with Casey and her dad, who'd always looked out for Rosalie when she was a kid. Casey met him for breakfast once a week just to check in and make sure he was doing okay, and Rosalie tried to join them when she could. Having a surrogate dad beat having no dad, or a mean, drunk one.

She was still working on her relationship with him. As predicted, hanging out with Benny had been a slippery slope that led to "just a beer here and there, socially," then skipped AA meetings, and then belligerent arguments that Rosalie had to just walk away from, grateful she wasn't living at home anymore.

He claimed he was sober again now, and Rosalie was working on trusting him.

"Your boss has you driving all over town chasing stories," Casey's dad said. "How many miles have you put on it in the last year alone?"

"Not sure," Rosalie fibbed. She had to submit expense reports for all her travel and she knew exactly how many miles she'd driven around Hickory Harbor in the last year. Far more than she thought possible for a city that was only about a third of the size of NYC.

She was steadily working her way through every major component under the Civic's hood, replacing each piece as it wore out, but she'd been driving it since high school. It seemed worth the trouble.

"It's got sentimental value," she pointed out.

"Your grandmother willed you that car because she wanted you to have some independence," Casey pointed out so helpfully, "but I'm sure if she could weigh in now, she'd want you to be safe."

Her dad nodded. "I worry about you breaking down on the highway – it's dangerous."

"I won't break down because I've replaced everything under the hood at least once." Rosalie checked the time on her phone. "I have to get going – I have an interview in thirty minutes. Thanks for breakfast."

"Anytime, sweetie."

"Bye, Rose," Casey said with a hug.

Rosalie left ten dollars on the table for the tip and took a to-go cup of coffee from the server, then went outside and hopped in the ancient Civic, which roared to life without hesitation. She patted the dashboard and cooed, "Who's my trusty old beater? You are!"

Her interview was with the developer of a massive medical complex going into what used to be the factory district downtown. He'd offered to give her a tour of the partially constructed building so he could demonstrate the scale of the place, and Rosalie had jumped at the opportunity for a more interesting interview than just sitting in some executive's office like usual.

When she arrived, construction was in full swing, with a bunch of different crews hard at work around the site.

A man in a suit and tie and an immaculate white hard hat waved to her, then pointed to a parking space next to an equally spotless Mercedes. Rosalie parked, then got out to meet him.

"Ira Greenstone?"

"That's me, and you must be Miss West from the Gazette."

Rosalie pointed to the ID badge she'd clipped to the collar of her blouse. "Rosalie, nice to meet you."

He handed her a hard hat, then swept his arm grandly at the construction going on around them. "Let me show you around the future home of the best health-care facilities in the state."

He talked – bragged – for nearly an hour without stopping, and Rosalie had to interrupt just to sneak a few questions in here and there. She recorded him with her phone as he marched her around the construction site, taking her inside the buildings that were safe to enter and pointing out where various departments would be located.

"It's going to be a major economic boon to this city, and the Gazette is welcome to come back anytime to see what we're doing for the community," he said as they were wrapping up and heading back toward their cars.

"How many jobs do you expect to create?"

It was one of only about five questions Rosalie had managed to ask, but she never got the answer because just then, someone screamed, "Oh shit!" accompanied by what sounded like an explosion very nearby.

That was not the sort of thing you wanted to hear when you were traipsing around a construction site in a skirt and a flimsy hard hat. Rosalie's eyes went wide, searching for the problem, and in the same instant she felt arms closing around her shoulders, yanking her backward. Everything was chaos and kicked up dust and construction workers shouting, and when her brain caught up to the present again, she found that Ira had pulled her to the safety of a half-completed lobby inside the nearest building.

"What happened?" she asked.

"I'm about to find out," he said, looking equal parts concerned and irritated that this had happened with a reporter on scene. "Stay here," he told her, but when he went outside, Rosalie's reporting instincts made her follow.

And she immediately wished she hadn't.

As the dust settled, her mouth dropped. The pristine white Mercedes sat exactly where it had been, not quite as clean as before but entirely untouched. And beside it, where her trusty old Civic used to be, there was a vaguely familiar red pancake crushed beneath a steel I-beam.

"Oh my god," she breathed.

"Stay where you are," Ira ordered. She wasn't sure if he was concerned about her safety or somehow thought he could hide the fact that her car had been flattened. Either way, he turned away from her and barked at his nearest employee, "What the hell happened?"

"Cable snapped," the guy said. "Just a freak accident. We did everything by the book."

"My car..." Rosalie was in a daze, unable to believe her eyes. Her work laptop had been in there, and the cassette tapes she'd carefully curated from thrift shops because the car still had a tape deck... Not to mention she was now stuck here with no ride to work.

"Thank god no one was injured," Ira said as he made his way back to her. "Can you imagine if we'd wrapped up the interview just a couple minutes earlier?"

Ira had already switched into spin mode, trying to

make her see the bright side of the situation – probably worried she'd sue for inviting her to tour a death trap. Right now, though, she was far too stunned to be angry.

"I left my coffee in there…"

It was a dumb thing to say and she knew it, but Ira sprang into action, barking orders. Seconds later, a cardboard to-go cup was being pressed into Rosalie's hand.

"It's construction site coffee, which means it was brewed at the foreman's house at five this morning and definitely won't be the best cup you've ever had, but it's caffeine," he said with a nervous chuckle. "Miss West, we're going to make this right, don't you worry, okay? Now, can I drive you somewhere? To a car rental agency, perhaps?"

He let out another chuckle and guided her toward the Mercedes. Rosalie cradled the lukewarm coffee in her hands and stared at the remains of her car as Ira pulled out of the lot.

She had him take her to the Gazette, just a five-minute drive. She went robotically to her desk and set down the untouched coffee. Ordinarily she'd plug in her laptop, check her email, start working up a to-do list for the day. This morning she had no computer to log into and she was working out how she was going to get home that afternoon.

She could call Casey for a ride, but what about tomorrow? And all the driving she did to talk to sources?

Her boss came by a couple minutes later while Rosalie was still staring at the empty space on her desk where her laptop should be. "How'd the interview go this morning?" He caught sight of the look in her eyes and frowned. "Whoa, you okay?"

"My car just got pulverized. Casey's dad's going to be so happy."

SAGE

THE PRESENT

The night Sage proposed, she and Rosalie spent the evening wrapped up in each other. They completely forgot about each other's big news, and mostly forgot about the food Sage had ordered.

They made love. They opened a bottle of champagne that Sage had chilling in the refrigerator, tucked behind a gallon of milk so Rosalie wouldn't see it before she was supposed to. And they curled up on the couch with Bear and a nest's worth of pillows and blankets.

Sage wrapped both arms around Rosalie, burying her face in the warm curve of her neck and breathing in her scent. Floral and comforting, it was a perfume she loved waking up to each morning and she was going to get to do that every day for the rest of her life. She squeezed Rosalie a little harder.

"How did I get so lucky?"

"Well, about a year and a half ago, somebody dropped a steel beam on my car. I had to buy a new car, and because it was not a junk heap like the last one, I started parking it in the car port behind my apartment whenever I could."

"The garbage-collecting car port, to go with your basically condemned apartment," Sage chimed in.

Rosalie nodded. "Where all the mice lived, and decided to upgrade their winter home to my engine block."

"And the rest is history."

Rosalie laughed. "So really, the question is how did I get so unlucky?"

Sage squeezed her again. "To get stuck with me."

"Luckiest bad luck I've ever had."

She leaned forward to retrieve her champagne from the coffee table – it was in a regular old drinking glass, a detail Sage had overlooked when she was planning the day.

"As soon as I'm good enough, I'm going to make you a set of champagne flutes," she promised.

"I'm sure you're good enough now, that rose is stunning," Rosalie said. "I think I'm going to take it to work on Monday and put it on my desk next to Wally so everyone can admire it – along with my beautiful ring, of course."

Sage lifted Rosalie's free hand, kissing her knuckles just below the glimmering hematite ring. Bear popped his head up from where he was curled beside them, sensing that affections were being shared at the other end of the couch. He bounded up to them, trying to lick everything he could reach.

"Not the lips," Sage laughed, burying her face against Rosalie's chest, "I draw the line at my lips!"

"Yep, those are all mine," Rosalie said, creating a protective cage around Sage's head with her arms while Bear went nuts trying to win this new game they'd inadvertently created. After a minute, Sage reached under the couch and fished out a tennis ball, tossing it to the far corner of the room.

Bear was off the couch like a shot, his paws skittering over the hardwood as he slid into the dining area and sank his teeth into the ball.

"Bring it here," Rosalie called.

Bear came running back, but that was where the concept of fetch fell apart for him. When she told him to drop it, he just kept chewing, giving her a look like, *come and take it if you want it so bad.*

"We really need to work on that," Sage laughed, reaching down to wrest the ball from his jaws.

She managed after a couple seconds' struggle, chucking the ball back across the room over her shoulder.

"Oh no!" Rosalie gasped.

"What?"

Sage turned to see her rogue throw bounce off the dining table. She winced, but everything remained intact.

Until Bear took that as an invitation to vault up one of the chairs and across the table in hot pursuit.

A second later, there was the sound of shattering glass and Sage and Rosalie were both scrambling to keep him away from the rose he'd knocked to the floor.

"I'll hold him, you get the broom," Rosalie said,

scooping Bear up and letting him smother her with doggy kisses.

"Shit, I am so sorry," Sage said as she went about cleaning up.

"Is it salvageable?"

Sage just laughed. "Pulverized."

"Aww, babe."

Rosalie came over to inspect the damage, then pulled Sage away from the cleanup effort when she saw the tears welling in her eyes.

"Come here, give us a hug."

She wrapped her arm around Sage, sandwiching Bear between them.

"That was supposed to be your forever rose. I can't believe I did that."

"It was an accident, and Bear says he's sorry."

"I'm sorry my aim is terrible," Sage answered. "I'll make you a hundred more roses to make up for this one."

"All I need is you, babe. You're all that matters."

17

ROSALIE

They announced their engagement slowly over the course of a couple of weeks, not being the big, flashy engagement party types. Sage's parents were the first to know because of their standing weekly dinners, and then Rosalie's dad.

She met him for coffee one evening to give him the news, and she didn't bring Sage with her because she wasn't sure what condition he'd be in. He said he was happy for them, but then he said he had to go meet up with Benny to help him clean out his gutters and he didn't stay long.

Of course, Casey was more fun to tell. As soon as Rosalie texted her a picture of her newly adorned ring finger, Casey decided to shout it from the metaphorical rooftops. She blasted it all over social media, and that was the end of the slow announcement idea.

And then the wedding planning chaos began in earnest.

The following week when they went to Sage's parents' house for dinner, there was an unexpected guest waiting for them.

"This is Stella," Sage's mom made the introductions, all smiles. "She works with me at the bank, but she's also a... wait for it..." Sage and Rosalie exchanged confused looks. "Wedding planner!"

"Oh. Mom, we were going to take care of the planning ourselves," Sage explained. "It's just going to be a small wedding, so–"

"You *were*," her mom said. "But you only get married once, and having a professional to guide you will take so much of the stress off your shoulders."

"I'll make sure you have the perfect wedding," Stella said, extending her hand to shake with both of them.

"And don't worry about the expense," Sage's mom said. "Stella is our gift to you."

Rosalie's chest twinged – they'd only been engaged two weeks and it was true she had no clue what went into planning a wedding, but she'd been looking forward to finding out with Sage.

On the other hand, one of the biggest things she'd noticed about Sage's mother in the year she'd known her was how dedicated she was to helping both her children. And she really was helpful.

Stress had a tendency to exacerbate any mental health problems Sage was having. Rosalie had seen that first-hand when Bear ate one of her socks and they'd had to spend a harrowing twenty-four hours waiting for him to pass it. The mental confusion and accompanying slow speech Sage had been so self-conscious of when they first started dating made a reappearance, and Rosalie could hardly tear her away from looking up worst-case scenarios on her phone.

If letting Stella help them plan their wedding would keep Sage's stress levels down, maybe it was for the best.

"Well, thank you, Angela, that's very thoughtful," Rosalie said, then turned to Stella. "How long have you been a wedding planner?"

Stella spotted Sage's dad coming into the room with a pitcher of iced tea. "Oh, drinks, I'd love one."

That evasion should have been a warning of how the whole process would go. But everything about the last couple of weeks – not to mention the last ten minutes – had been overwhelming, so Rosalie didn't notice. She just accepted a glass of iced tea and slipped her hand into Sage's as they headed toward the dining room.

"You okay with this?" Sage whispered to her.

"I'm not sure we have a choice, babe." She said it with a smile and a peck on Sage's cheek.

"Sorry," Sage answered, pinching an entirely different cheek just before they stepped through the doorway to join the others.

Dinner was pork chops and fresh greens, and Stella dominated the meal with all her ideas for the wedding. She was chipper to a fault and Rosalie couldn't imagine how excited she'd be if she were planning her own wedding, because she was at least an eight out of ten on the excitement scale on account of their wedding.

Even Rosalie wasn't *that* pumped about flower arrangements.

As soon as the dinner plates were off the table, Stella hauled a massive binder out of her tote bag and thumped it down in front of them, pulling her chair around so she could wedge herself between Sage and Rosalie. "I took the liberty to pull together a few mood boards for inspiration."

A few, Sage mouthed to Rosalie behind Stella's head, eyes wide at the size of the binder. It was stuffed from front to back with magazine cutouts, catering menus, and local business cards.

Rosalie stifled a chuckle as she leaned forward to see what Stella had come up with.

"Crimson is always a classic color choice."

"Mm, I don't know if bright red is really *us*," Rosalie said.

"Not bright red, *crimson*." Stella said the word as if it were the most exquisite color in existence. She looked between the two of them, saw the skepticism in their eyes and frowned. She turned the page to a new collage. "Blush pink is in vogue, and very feminine."

"I, on the other hand, am not the most feminine of brides," Sage answered. She gestured at the navy plaid shirt and men's-cut Dockers she was wearing as proof. "I don't know about Rosalie, but I was thinking of a more neutral color palette, maybe something nature-inspired?"

Stella's eyes flared as if she was trying very hard to swallow down a revulsion for neutral color palettes. "It's your big day. You want to be flashy so that all eyes are on you…" She started flipping pages again, murmuring mostly to herself, "I don't think I even have any inspiration photos that bland."

"Not bland, just neutral," Sage said.

Her mom came back from the kitchen with a pot of coffee and an apple pie, and Sage sent her a *help us* look.

"Neutral tones are nice," Angela said, setting down the pie. "What about your namesake, a nice sage green?"

"Oh, I have some greens," Stella brightened, flipping to a page full of bridesmaids in dresses that were more on the emerald end of the spectrum. "These are pretty," she said hopefully.

"Why don't we put a pin in the color scheme for now and talk about venues?" Rosalie suggested.

"Something outdoors," Sage suggested, and in the same breath, Stella said, "A high-end banquet hall."

Rosalie couldn't help it – this time she did laugh out loud, in a combination of frustration and amusement.

"You don't want an outdoor wedding," Stella informed them, sticking a Post-it note to the emerald-green mood board before she flipped to the *Venues* section of her binder. "There are far too many variables – the weather, insects, grass stains on your dresses, and you'd have to book your caterer and rent all the furniture separately. Banquet halls are all-inclusive."

"Well, we could at least take a look," Angela compromised for them. "What hall do you think would be best, Stella?"

Sage leaned back in her chair so she could roll her eyes behind Stella's back, mouthing *sorry* to Rosalie. Rosalie just stuck her tongue out, finding amusement in the situation – for now.

SAGE

"**A**re you *sure* you don't want me to fire her? Because I will." Sage had made that offer at least a half-dozen times by now.

They'd spent the last three months working with Stella on planning their wedding – or more accurately, planning Stella's ideal wedding. Every interaction went pretty much the same as that first meeting. They disagreed with her on everything from the venue type to the guest favors, and Stella dug her heels in every single time.

"Jordan almonds are a classic for a reason – they're traditional, inexpensive, and symbolic. Your guests will expect them."

"I still like the idea of handing out wildflower seed packets," Rosalie had argued. "They're also inexpensive and symbolic, and does anybody really *like* Jordan almonds?"

"Plus, isn't the symbolism that an almond looks

vaguely like an egg?" Sage asked with a snort. "Pretty sure we're not getting any fertility luck without professional intervention."

"They're also for health, wealth, happiness and longevity," Stella ticked off on her fingers. "So if you want to be sick, poor, sad and die young, sure, skip the almonds."

They told her she could order the Jordan almonds. Then when she was gone, Sage told Rosalie they'd also order seed packets – Stella wouldn't have to know.

That was how a lot of the wedding planning had gone, and Sage really wouldn't have minded giving Stella the boot. She was a nice woman, and extremely enthusiastic about her job, but there was no love lost between them.

"I don't want to start our marriage off by offending your mother," Rosalie said today as they arrived at the bridal boutique. It was dress shopping day, and this was the same argument she'd made every time Sage offered to get rid of Stella. "Besides, she's difficult to work with but she *is* taking a lot off our plate."

"Okay, but if she tries to put me in some poofy tulle thing, I can't be accountable for what I do."

Inside the boutique, Willow and Casey were waiting patiently as the two members of the bridal party, as well as Sage's mom. "Where's Stella?" Sage asked, surprised she wasn't the first to greet them as they came through the door.

Her mom opened her mouth to answer, but before she could even form the words, the excitable wedding planner burst through a dense rack of wedding gowns with two garment bags thrown over her arm. "There you two are! I couldn't help myself, I started without you."

Rosalie glanced at her smartwatch and murmured under her breath, "We're ten minutes early for our appointment."

"Stella has been picking out gowns for you two for fifteen minutes already," Willow said, wry amusement in her tone.

"I hope you're in the mood to try things on because she's already nearly filled a whole dressing room," their saleswoman said, trailing Stella out of the racks with another dress in her arms. "I'm Laura, by the way."

"Hi," Rosalie shook her free hand.

"Actually, I was thinking of a nice, tailored suit," Sage said.

Stella looked like she'd been slapped.

"We'll make sure everyone gets exactly what they want," Laura said. "I understand we're looking for bridesmaid gowns today too?"

"We're running short on time as it is!" Stella answered, coming back from the dressing room. "I've been planning my own wedding for *years* and these two are trying to get it all done in six months."

"When's your wedding?" Laura asked.

"Oh, just as soon as I find Mr. Right. Which will be any day now, I hope!" A rare frown crossed Stella's face, but then she was right back to her mission. "So, Rosalie and Sage, let me show you the gowns I picked out!"

They were all extremely full-skirted with long trains

and lots of shimmering beadwork. Rosalie was as polite as possible when she explained that her own style was more Bohemian, lacy, and slim-profiled, but Sage couldn't help being blunt when Stella suggested she try on a bejeweled gown with a plunging neckline that looked like it had come straight off the red carpet.

"I'd rather walk down the aisle naked," she said, pushing it away as Stella held it out to her.

"That is a beautiful dress for a very different bride," Laura said diplomatically. "You, maybe, when Mr. Right comes along."

"Oh no, I've had my wedding dress picked out since the moment I saw the latest Vera Wang collection. Please, just try it, Sage – it might surprise you."

"I assure you, it will not."

"Stella, Sage has never been the dress-wearing type," her mom tried to help.

"I'll try it on," Rosalie said, and before Stella could mount any further protest, she took the gown out of her hands. "Sage, come into the dressing room and help me."

Sage could use a Stella time-out so she eagerly followed her fiancée into the room, along with Laura. "Thank you," she said the moment the door was closed. "Can I fire her now?"

Rosalie sighed. "Maybe we should."

"Not seeing eye-to-eye with the wedding planner?" Laura asked as she slipped the gown off its hanger and helped Rosalie step into it.

"Do you see that a lot?"

Laura chuckled. "I don't often see wedding planners coming to dress appointments."

She directed Rosalie to stand on the platform in the center of the room and used garment clips to secure the back of the sample dress, a few sizes too big for her. There were mirrors on three of the walls, and Sage enjoyed looking at her from multiple angles.

"That dress actually does look good on you – makes your chest look fabulous."

Rosalie laughed. "I'm not sure I want such a busty dress. Our parents are going to be at the wedding."

"We couldn't pick this one just on the principle of the thing anyway," Sage said.

"So what do we do about Stella?"

"I'm still for firing her," Sage answered.

Rosalie frowned.

"What?"

"She's just... kinda pathetic? I feel bad saying that, but I'd feel worse firing her."

"So let me do it," Sage said.

Rosalie just smirked, then shook her head. "Let's give her another chance. What if Mr. Right never comes along and planning other people's weddings is all she gets?"

Sage stepped onto the platform with Rosalie, careful not to step on the extravagant train pooling around her feet. She cupped her face and gave her a quick kiss. "You are a bleeding heart and I love you for it."

When they emerged from the dressing room, Stella absolutely lost her shit at the sight of the red carpet dress.

"It's perfect! You *have* to get that one!" She turned to

Sage. "And you were right – this dress is made for Rosalie. Don't you worry, we'll find another one for you."

They were in the boutique for five hours, and would have stayed longer if it hadn't closed. By the end, everyone was exhausted except for Stella, who had just as much energy as she did at the beginning of the appointment.

She'd managed to wrangle Sage into a couple of dresses, but only after she tried on a few sleek white suits and found one she loved. And Sage would rather die than admit it, but the white satin heels that Stella had shoved her way actually looked damn good with the suit she'd chosen.

Casey and Willow found chiffon bridesmaids' dresses that they liked, and Rosalie, Sage and Stella all liked them too – it was a wedding planning miracle and Stella didn't even pout too much when they ordered the dresses in moss green.

Rosalie found an absolutely stunning gown that was the perfect compromise between the Bohemian style that she liked and the more formal style that Stella insisted would go with their banquet hall venue... and when Laura told them the price, Sage watched the color drain right out of Rosalie's face.

It was more than they'd planned to spend on the entire wedding.

"Rose, I really wish I could help you out," Casey said. "I just helped my dad buy a new refrigerator after his old one died..."

"No, I wouldn't let you chip in anyway. This is just

too extravagant," Rosalie said, obviously suppressing a frown as she ran her hands over the fine lace on her hips. "We're not five-figure wedding dress people, something simpler will do just fine."

Sage hated seeing her take that dress off – for one because it really was beautiful on her, and two, because she could see the heartbreak on Rosalie's face, no matter how hard she tried to hide it.

In the end, Rosalie placed an order for her second-favorite dress, something that was a little more *Downton Abbey* and a little less free-spirited, but that she looked gorgeous in nonetheless.

She could have put a Hefty bag over her head and Sage would still think she was the most beautiful woman in the world, of course, but this was a definite step up from a trash bag.

And Sage got her way when it came to the suit – not because Stella backed down, but because Sage proved just as stubborn.

"I'm going to change your mind about this," Stella promised as she hovered over Sage's shoulder while Laura filled out the order form for the suit. "Mark my words."

"You'd sooner see me walking down the aisle in lederhosen than a wedding gown," Sage shot right back at her. She waited till Stella got distracted by the veils, then quietly asked Laura to add those satin heels to her order.

19

ROSALIE

S itting down at her desk the Monday morning after dress shopping day felt like a vacation to Rosalie.

She was having serious doubts about her decision to keep going to bat for Stella. The woman was, to put it mildly, *a lot*, and sometimes Rosalie wondered if they were actually saving Sage from the stress of wedding planning when Stella brought stress with her wherever she went.

They were already three months into the planning, though, and with the wardrobe selections out of the way, they were one decision closer to the wedding. Maybe they were over the worst of it now and the rest would just be small details that wouldn't be so bad to tussle with Stella over.

Rosalie was getting caught up on email and savoring her Monday morning chai latte when her boss sidled up to her desk.

"Come by my office whenever you have a minute," he said. "We need to talk about your column."

He left, and suddenly Rosalie was no longer on vacation.

She sat up straight and set her latte aside, heading to the newspaper's website to check on the latest installment of her community interest column. She'd been writing it for a quarter now, and she was proud of the work she was doing – but the way her boss said that, it sounded like it was about to be ripped out from under her.

Frowning, she searched for her byline and clicked on her most recent article. Inspired by the stories that Sage had told her about experiencing hospitalization and inter-acting with first responders during a mental health crisis, Rosalie had decided to go into the community and talk to those people.

Try to understand what it was like from both sides of the situation.

Find out how to make it easier for everyone.

Her articles weren't just relevant to people with schizophrenia and their doctors. Addiction, anxiety and depression, trauma and abuse, there were a lot of things that led to psychiatric emergencies – which Rosalie was learning right along with her readers – and everyone from paramedics and police to the patients' family members could benefit from better understanding the process.

It wasn't the column Rosalie's boss expected to get when he gave her the assignment, but it had been well-received.

Or so she thought.

She was deep in the task of scouring the comments sections of all twelve of her articles when her closest work friend, Troy, plopped his butt down on her desk.

"You're squishing Wally," she said, swatting at him with a notepad.

"What are you so focused on this early on a Monday?" he asked, ignoring her complaint.

"Hasan wants to talk to me about my column. I'm trying to figure out what's wrong with it."

"I thought people liked it."

"Me too," Rosalie grumbled.

"How did dress shopping go this weekend?" Troy asked. "Is your wedding planner still being a bridezilla?"

Rosalie snorted. "For sure. Sage and I found our outfits, though, and I don't think Casey or Willow are plotting our deaths over their bridesmaid gowns."

"Not that I would know a thing about wedding dresses – renting a tux to be a groomsman is pretty damn easy – but from what I've heard, that's about as successful as you can get."

"Yeah, I guess Stella did okay after all."

Troy looked over the top of Rosalie's low-walled cubicle in the direction of the boss's office. "Did Hasan say he wanted to talk to you right away? Cuz he's kinda glaring this way."

"Oh great, I better go."

Troy further rearranged her desk while getting off it and Rosalie took a minute to straighten it up, then stood tall and marched over to Hasan's office.

"Now a good time?"

"Sit down," he said, gesturing to the chairs across from his desk.

"I checked the comments and the stats on my last few articles," she said, switching into fight-for-your-column mode. "No negative comments, which is pretty rare on even the most benign article, and the view count is respectable."

"It's more than respectable," Hasan said, taking her aback.

"Oh yeah?"

"Every article in your column is better-read than the last," he said. "At this rate, it's on track to be the most popular column in the paper."

"Seriously?" Rosalie had to pick her jaw up off the ground.

"I've been getting appreciative calls and letters to the editor all month. People are really finding it informative and relatable."

"Well... that's great."

"I wanted to make sure you have enough content to keep it going for a while," Hasan said. "How long do you see this series running?"

Rosalie couldn't wipe the smile off her face. Sage had been reading along, giving her tips and ideas, and she was going to be so proud when Rosalie told her it was a hit. "Indefinitely," she said, "as long as people are interested. I have an interview scheduled with a psychiatric ER nurse for this week's article."

"Great, keep up the good work."

He turned his attention abruptly to his computer, signaling to Rosalie that she could go, and she left the office on a cloud.

"Good news?" Troy asked as she passed his desk.

"The column's a hit."

"You go, girl," he said, hand in the air. She slapped him a high five and kept going. Maybe today could be the vacation she was looking for after all.

20

SAGE

O n Monday evening, Sage left work early after replacing a catalytic converter – so much easier and faster now that she was working out of a proper garage with all the tools she could possibly need. She gave herself plenty of time to go home and wash off the grease, and was just coming back to the apartment after a walk with Bear when Rosalie pulled into the driveway.

"Hey babe, are you ready for registry shopping?" she said as they met at the door.

They had an appointment in half an hour, and it was one of the wedding planning tasks Rosalie had most been looking forward to.

"Don't get me wrong, I love our eclectic apartment full of odds and ends," she'd said when Stella reminded them about the task, "but it'd be really nice to have a toaster that doesn't blow a fuse every time we use it at the same time as the microwave."

She kissed Sage hello and then stooping to greet Bear

in a similar fashion – although the kiss was directed to the top of his head instead of his lips. "Does it make me materialistic that I'm excited about this?" she asked. "It's not like I want a bunch of expensive junk we won't use, but..."

"You're allowed to want matching plates," Sage laughed. "Come on, we'll give Bear his dinner and then go."

On the way to the store, Sage drove while Rosalie relayed the good news she'd gotten from her boss that morning.

"You're a fantastic reporter," Sage assured her, "I knew the column would be a success."

"It's just as much your doing as mine," Rosalie insisted. "You gave me the idea. I had no clue what mental health services were even available, let alone what it was like trying to access them. Apparently neither did the Gazette's readership, but it's important."

"I'm proud of you, babe," Sage said, reaching over to take Rosalie's hand. "And I appreciate you."

"Oh. My. God."

As they pulled into the parking lot, Sage felt Rosalie stiffen under her touch.

"What?"

"Look."

She pointed to a familiar mint-green VW Beetle with eyelashes over the headlights parked in front of the store.

"Uh, did Stella tell us she was coming to this appointment?" Sage asked.

"No... and I didn't tell her when it was."

"Well, maybe it's a coincidence," Sage said. "Maybe she's just shopping, or it isn't even her car."

"Do you think anyone else drives something like that?"

"I'll park on the other side of the lot just in case," Sage said.

"Avoiding our wedding planner. This is normal."

Sage chuckled. "I will not let her ruin this for you, I promise."

They went inside, looking around shiftily like a couple of criminals trying not to be spotted, and made their way to the guest services desk.

Where Stella was waiting for them, already holding the scanner.

"Oh boy, here we go," Rosalie said under her breath as they approached, smiles plastered on their faces.

"Stella, what are you doing here?" Sage asked through clenched teeth.

"Surprise! I did a little sleuthing and found out your appointment time."

Rosalie smiled stiffly. "Why?"

"I know you two just moved in together a few months ago and you probably don't even know what you'll need once you're married," Stella said, flourishing her free hand in a *tada* gesture. "But that's what I'm for."

"That's what the store consultant we made our appointment with is for," Rosalie pointed out.

"But she doesn't know you," Stella said. "I told her I could handle it. Now, China patterns – I was thinking of something classic but showy, since you'll only be using it for special occasions. Something like the Spode Blue Italian set–"

"Oh no!" Sage announced loudly, putting her hand to her stomach.

Rosalie and Stella looked at her wide-eyed.

"Diarrhea," she said loudly, "babe, we gotta go. Stella, I'm so sorry." Sage was already pulling Rosalie toward the exit, and Stella came stammering after them.

"There's a restroom around here somewhere–"

"Nope, 'fraid this is going to be an all-night problem, I can tell," Sage answered. "We'll reschedule, sorry, Stella!"

Rosalie caught on and by the time they got outside, they were both struggling not to laugh.

"Hold it in until we get to the car," Sage said, which only made Rosalie turn redder.

"You do the same," she teased.

As soon as they were safely locked in, with the windows rolled up, they both let go, howling at the horrified look on Stella's face.

"I can't believe you just announced to an entire Bed, Bath and Beyond that you have diarrhea," Rosalie said, then turned abruptly sentimental. "Aww, and you did it for me."

"I did it for both of us," Sage said, "but I will happily embarrass myself for your sake any day. I love you."

"I love you too." Rosalie glanced back toward the store, which Stella still hadn't come out of. "What do you think are the odds she goes ape with the scanner whether we're there or not?"

"Fifty-fifty, if I'm being generous. We'll come back next week and have the consultant give us a clean slate, then pick out our own stuff. I'm sorry she ruined tonight."

"Nothing is ruined," Rosalie said, then lunged over the shifter to shower Sage in kisses. "You're the perfect woman, you know that?"

"Even with my unpredictable bowels?"

Rosalie snorted, then gave Sage a wink. "Let's go home and I'll nurse you back to health."

21

ROSALIE

osalie was sitting at the dining room table the following night after work, frowning at her computer as she paid a couple utility bills.

They were doing okay – neither of them had a high-paying job, but they could support themselves, and so far they'd avoided the common trap of falling into debt for the sake of their wedding. No thanks to Stella, that was. She'd argued hard for a wedding gown for Rosalie that had five digits on the price tag, and she'd picked the nicest, priciest venue in town for the reception.

One silver lining there, the venue ended up cancelling, saying they'd double-booked the date. It was one more stressor added to the list, but Stella had pulled through and found them a backup venue for a little less money.

Sage was working more, taking on more clients and staying at the shop later. Part of it was excitement over having access to all the tools of a professional mechanic's shop, plus her clients loved her and she got all kinds of referrals from them. But Rosalie worried that Sage was biting off more than she could chew in an attempt to pay for some dream wedding that wasn't even that important in the long run.

Bear jumped onto Rosalie's lap, entirely obscuring her view of the laptop screen to make sure her attention was where it should be.

"Let me just..." Rosalie craned her neck around him to click submit on the electric bill payment, then closed the laptop. "There. It is now Bear Time, and hopefully your *otha motha* comes home soon and we can all play."

She scooped a rubber ball off the floor and chucked it the length of the apartment. Bear launched off her lap and went flying after it, nearly colliding with the wall as he snatched it and came running back.

And then back the other direction, skidding across the hardwood.

And back again.

"Drop it," Rosalie coached, but he just took off in another speed run, ball still firmly clenched between his jaws.

He'd never quite gotten the hang of fetch. Something about the fact that he had to let go of the ball in order to have it thrown again didn't click for him, no matter how many YouTube videos Rosalie and Sage watched to try to teach him.

She found another toy on the floor, a plushie shaped

like a pork chop, and squeaked it. "Bear, look what I have!"

She threw that one through the door to the bedroom. He forgot all about the ball, off on a new mission, and Rosalie checked the time. It was a little after six and before the wedding planning started, Sage used to get home from work before Rosalie pretty often. Now she was putting in long hours at the shop and Rosalie usually beat her home.

Hopefully that would change after the wedding, when they had fewer money worries.

Bear came tearing through the living room, the pork chop in his mouth, showing it off to Rosalie but not letting go. She retrieved the rubber ball where he'd abandoned it under the coffee table and threw it back in the other direction.

"Holy shit," Sage said, stepping through the kitchen door just as the ball went flying past her nose. "My life just flashed before my eyes."

"Incoming," Rosalie said belatedly, and Sage pulled up short to avoid tripping over the dog. He went scrambling under the dining table, and Rosalie scooped Sage up in a hug. "Despite the message chucking things at your head might send, I missed you so much."

"I'm not *too* late, am I?"

They kissed, and Rosalie said, "I was about to call the shop owner and ask him to kick you out."

"I'm sorry. Do you want to order takeout for dinner or should I cook to make it up to you?"

"I have a better idea," Rosalie said, dipping her head

and planting a couple kisses on Sage's neck. She felt her fiancée melt beneath her and let out a groan.

"I like that idea."

Rosalie gave a wicked chuckle. "Actually, that was just a tease... maybe a little bit of revenge for taking so long getting home." She nipped Sage's shoulder through her white T-shirt, then met her eyes again. "I think we should go out. It's been a long time since we did anything, just the two of us, no wedding planning."

"That idea's even better," Sage said, hands on Rosalie's hips. She pulled her closer, their bodies pressed firmly against each other, exacting her own sort of revenge as desire awoke in Rosalie's core. "What did you have in mind?"

"It's unseasonably warm out and it'll be light for another hour or so," Rosalie said. "Why don't we take Bear for a walk on the beach? We can eat at the pier. I heard there's a new banh mi food truck that's out of this world."

"Well, how could I resist that?"

They got Bear into his harness and Sage changed out of her grease-stained jeans and tee into a vintage knit sweater she'd scored from the thrift store last time they went. Rosalie stood in the bedroom doorway admiring her while she changed, noticing the subtle muscle definition of her arms.

"You're getting swole from so much extra time at the shop."

Sage looked at her biceps, grinned, and flexed for

Rosalie. "Don't worry, babe, your ticket to the gun show will always be comped."

Rosalie laughed and shook her head. "Let's go – I want my sandwich before I fill up on all that cheese."

The pier was crowded with couples on dates and families enjoying the nice weather. There was a mix of food trucks and sit-down restaurants, depending on what end of the pier you were on, as well as little boutiques, an arcade, a coffee shop and a few bike and surfboard rental shops. It was only a fifteen-minute drive from the apartment and Bear loved the water, so it was a go-to destination when they had the time.

Which hadn't been for a while, between the winter weather and the wedding planning. Bear started tugging on his lead as soon as he got out of the car.

"We're going, we're going!" Sage promised, double wrapping the leash around her hand. "How can a twenty-five-pound dog pull so hard?"

"He's got the stubbornness of a Weimaraner."

"More like a whiner-aner."

"Do you want to take him down to the beach?" Rosalie asked, grabbing the towel they kept in the back of the car just for Bear. "I can get our food and meet you down there."

"Nah. Sorry, Bear, but you need to learn patience," Sage said.

They found the banh mi truck and ordered a couple sandwiches, then followed a short wood plank path down to the beachfront. This area wasn't too crowded since it was past seven and the water was still pretty cold given the time of year.

Bear didn't mind in the least, though. When they reached the off-leash area and Sage let him go, he tore through the sand and launched himself into the icy water.

"Think he's gonna be over it as soon as he realizes it's cold?" Rosalie asked as she handed Sage her sandwich.

"No way, he's living his best life right now."

Indeed, the whole time they were eating their dinner, Bear splashed through the water without a care in the world. He zoomed through the sand here and there, and periodically checked to make sure his people were still there, but he was having a blast.

Sage wrapped her arm around Rosalie as soon as she was done eating, resting her head on her shoulder. "This was a great idea. I've missed this."

"The beach?"

"Spending quality time with you. Not that planning the wedding isn't important, but..." Sage trailed off and Rosalie nodded.

"I know what you mean. I've always heard it's stressful, but I never imagined it'd be like this." Rosalie let out a sigh. "Just a couple more months and we're home free. We've got most of the big stuff done by now."

Sage lifted her head. "Is that awful? That we're counting the months until we're married because we want it over with?"

Rosalie thought for a minute. Was it?

"No," she decided. "It's not like either of us ever

wanted a big, fairytale wedding. We just want to be married."

"We should go down to city hall tomorrow and just do it," Sage mused, but Rosalie snorted.

"We've come too far."

2 2

SAGE

They were on their way back to the car with a damp, sandy, but sleepy and satisfied Bear when they walked past a vintage clothing boutique at the end of the pier. That sort of thing barely registered in Sage's mind – she saw girly stuff in the window and just kept right on going. It took her a couple of paces before she realized her fiancée was no longer beside her.

She turned around to find Rosalie staring wistfully at the window display, and Sage gave a chuckle.

"Find something good?"

"It's beautiful," Rosalie breathed, drawing one hand down the glass.

Sage and Bear circled back and she slipped her arm around Rosalie's waist. She had her eyes locked on a knee-length white dress on a dress form in the window. It had delicately embroidered lace and beaded accents, and the skirt was flowing and beachy, perfect for the pier.

"You should try it on," Sage suggested.

Rosalie's brow furrowed. "What for?"

Sage shrugged. "Fun?"

"It looks like a wedding dress," Rosalie pointed out. "I already ordered mine."

"You looked stunning in that dress, but your eyes didn't light up in it like they did just now," Sage pointed out. She pushed Rosalie toward the boutique door. "Seriously – go try it on. For me. Bear and I will wait out here cuz I doubt the owner wants a sandy dog in their store."

Rosalie went inside and Sage found a bench to sit on not far from the door. She did her best to dry Bear off more with the towel – it was pretty amazing how stubbornly his short fur held on to water any time they went to the beach or took a walk in the rain.

"Babe?"

Sage looked up, and Rosalie was stepping out of the boutique in the dress. It fit her perfectly, elegantly hugging every curve, and she'd never been more beautiful.

"What do you think?" Rosalie asked.

"Hot *damn*," Sage said, standing and nearly dropping Bear's leash.

Rosalie chuckled, and Sage noticed that the shop owner had come outside with her. Probably trying to make sure she didn't take off down the pier with her merchandise, but she was also grinning from ear to ear.

"I happen to agree," the woman said, "this dress was made for her. Well, technically it was made in the fifties for another lucky woman, but it's been beautifully preserved since then, and clearly it was just waiting for you."

Rosalie did a happy little spin, the skirt fanning out around her. "I really like it."

"We'll take it," Sage said, already reaching for her wallet.

"No," Rosalie objected, "we won't."

"But it's perfect," Sage said.

"I already have a wedding dress, and I have nowhere else fancy enough to wear this," Rosalie said. She turned to the boutique owner. "It's gorgeous and I appreciate you letting me try it on. I hope some lucky bride finds it and loves it as much as I do."

Sage wanted to insist, but a nagging voice in the back of her head was a little relieved when Rosalie wouldn't let her. She hadn't even asked how much the dress cost, and they were already struggling with all the other expenses...

Still, it was a damn shame. She hadn't seen Rosalie this glowingly happy since the day she proposed.

Rosalie turned toward the boutique, ready to take the dress off, then second-guessed herself and whipped back around, throwing her arms around Sage. "I love this dress, but I love you so much more and you're all I need for the perfect wedding day."

23

ROSALIE

When they got home, Sage was busy rattling off their evening to-do list.

"I did my best with the beach towel, but Bear's still all gritty with sand so he needs a bath, and I almost forgot the bills are due today, and–"

Rosalie cornered her in the kitchen, bracing her hands against the counter on either side of Sage's hips. "I already paid the bills."

"Oh yeah?" The corner of Sage's mouth turned up as she recognized the desire in Rosalie's eyes, in the tone of her voice.

"And Bear can wait just a little bit longer. I have something else on my mind right now." Rosalie circled her arms around Sage, pulling her close, kissing her hard.

"Is this your way of saying thank you for the night out?" Sage teased.

"It's my way of telling you that I screwed up earlier," Rosalie said. Sage gave her a confused look, so she explained. "I thought I was teasing you before we left, kissing you and getting all feisty. But I played myself. I've been worked up ever since."

She ran her fingers through Sage's short hair, letting her fingertips glide softly over the back of her neck and along her earlobe, where she knew Sage was sensitive.

Sage reached down wordlessly to unclip Bear's leash and he went racing into the next room. Then she turned her attention wholly to Rosalie, an urgent hunger in her eyes. Her hands went to the hem of Rosalie's shirt, and soon they were in a frenzy of desire, pulling each other's clothes off and flinging them all over the kitchen floor.

Sage's hands went to Rosalie's bare breasts, and she gasped at the touch. Her thumbs circled Rosalie's nipples, flicking and teasing them until they were hard and aching. She'd had every intention of ravishing Sage, taking control and seeing to her every need...

But with the warmth of Sage's breath on her neck and the sensation of her hands over her breasts creating a tingling sensation all the way down between her legs, Rosalie gave herself over to Sage.

Her whole body ached and throbbed with need, and Sage knew just what to do.

God, she was so good at this.

Sage's hand worked its way down to her stomach, and then beneath the waistband of Rosalie's panties. Her thighs started to tremble and Sage turned her around, pressing her against the counter just as her fingers slid into the wetness between Rosalie's thighs.

"Have you been this wet for me all night?" Sage

murmured against Rosalie's ear, sending a rush of desire up through her cheeks and all the way to the top of her head.

"Yes," Rosalie breathed. "I almost didn't even tell you about my idea to go to the beach."

"I'm glad we went," Sage said in between nibbles on Rosalie's neck and the shell of her ear. "But I'm even more glad we're back now."

Her fingers teased Rosalie's clit while she talked and palmed her throbbing pussy like she was claiming it.

All yours, Rosalie thought dizzily, *I'm all yours.*

Then Sage's hand abruptly left her panties, and Rosalie sighed with the loss. Then her breath caught in her throat as Sage dropped to her knees in front of her and dragged Rosalie's damp panties down to her ankles.

She brought her hands back up to Rosalie's thighs, squeezing the curves of her ass as she buried her face between her legs.

"Oh fuck," she groaned, gripping the countertop behind her. Sage's tongue explored her, tasting her juices and rolling over her clit. "I'm close already."

"You're all worked up for me, I know, baby," Sage murmured against her skin. "Come on my tongue, I want to taste you."

The dirty talk made blood rush into Rosalie's cheeks, and she let go of the counter so she could run her fingers through Sage's soft blonde hair and guide her mouth where she needed it.

Right there.

Sage's tongue found the sweet spot, increasing the pressure as she sensed Rosalie tensing up.

"Yes…" she breathed, hands fisting in Sage's hair.

Her thighs started to shake uncontrollably and Sage wrapped her arms more firmly around Rosalie's ass, pinning her in place as she came against her mouth.

Everything faded away for a few heartbeats, and when Rosalie came back to herself, Sage was standing up, encircling Rosalie in her arms and kissing her.

"You're so fucking sexy."

"Me? That was all you, baby. I'm not sure I can even move my legs right now," Rosalie said. Her thighs were still quivering slightly and she was leaning against the counter for support.

"Well then, I'll just have to carry you to the bedroom, because I'm not done with you yet," Sage said, kissing and sucking a teasing path along her neck.

"I suddenly have the strength to walk," Rosalie mumbled, eyes fluttering closed as a new wave of desire crashed over her. "I just needed the motivation."

Sage took her hand, pulling her naked through the living room to their bedroom on the other side of the apartment. They raced quickly past the big picture window with its curtains open, and Rosalie spared a quick glance around to locate Bear. He was on the couch, contentedly gnawing on a bully stick and completely oblivious to his humans' activities.

Rosalie took the lead, chasing Sage into the bedroom and throwing her down on the bed, then pouncing on her. "This is more like what I had in mind."

"Oh yeah, what are you gonna do to me?" Sage challenged, her eyes full of fire and lust.

Rosalie grabbed Sage's wrists, pinning them at her sides. "Whatever. I. Want."

She draped herself over Sage, enjoying the way their bodies molded together as they kissed. She couldn't help grinding her hips a little, sending little shivers of pleasure through her.

Right now, though, it was about Sage.

Rosalie crawled off her, whole body aching with the need for more of this incredible woman. She reached over to the bedside table and pulled out the drawer, where a growing collection of toys were waiting for them.

Rosalie loved it when Sage used the strap-on, pressing her knees up into her chest so she could thrust deep inside her. Just the sight of the crimson leather harness and the small but powerful silicone toy that went with it made Rosalie wet all over again, thinking of how hot Sage looked in it.

Her hand traveled over the strap-on, though, to Sage's favorite toy.

She wasn't fancy, her hand did the job just fine – that was what Sage told Rosalie when they first started dating. And it did. Even a touch as simple as Sage's finger brushing over Rosalie's bare arm was enough to send a shiver through her, and the sex was phenomenal without any supplements at all.

But toys could be fun, and Rosalie had talked Sage into branching out a little bit. And then a bit more.

It turned out Sage loved the variety as much as

Rosalie hoped she would, and by now their little collection filled most of the drawer. And the big surprise was that Sage's favorite thing was the one she'd been the most reluctant to try.

Rosalie took out the narrow silicone butt plug, and Sage's eyes flared when she saw it. Nibbling on her lower lip, she watched Rosalie crawl down between her legs.

She lay down on her belly, one arm hooking around Sage's thigh as she kissed and then licked her clit, and parted her folds. Sage was glistening with need already, and Rosalie ran the plug up and down over her slit, using her juices to lubricate it. She pushed it into her pussy a few times while she sucked and licked Sage's clit, enjoying the chorus of moans and the undulations of her body with every thrust.

Rosalie took her time, making sure to tease and pleasure Sage until her moans reached a fever pitch. Then she looked up at her. "Ready?"

"So fucking ready."

Rosalie gently worked the plug into Sage's ass, slowly easing it in until it was fully seated, then waiting a moment – to let Sage adjust to it, but mostly just to torture her a little bit more.

Then she lowered her mouth to Sage's clit, laving it with urgency this time as she periodically pressed on the base of the plug, moving it subtly and making Sage squirm.

"*Ohmygodohfuckyes.*"

Rosalie always knew when Sage was about to tip over the edge when she lost the ability to speak in sentences.

139

Rosalie grinned to herself as she continued to lick and suck, and pushed her thumb into Sage's core so she could keep manipulating the plug with her other fingers.

"*HolyshitI'mgonnacome...*"

Sage clapped her thighs around Rosalie's ears and her whole body convulsed against her, the plug heightening the sensations until she was nothing more than a writhing ball of ecstasy. Rosalie stopped moving, keeping the plug pressed firmly against Sage's opening to let her ride out the orgasm, until at last Sage went limp.

Rosalie grinned up at her. "Good?"

"*Fuck,*" Sage panted in response. "I love you."

"Me or the plug?" Rosalie teased.

"Can't it be both?"

Rosalie chuckled, then carefully eased the plug out and set it on the nightstand. They'd get cleaned up in a few minutes, but right now all she wanted was to curl up next to Sage, her head resting on the softness of her breast, listening as her heartbeat returned to normal.

24

SAGE

During work the next day, Sage was still daydreaming – not just about the sex but the impromptu date night on the pier and the way Rosalie's eyes lit up at that vintage dress. It was a good thing the most complicated thing Sage had in her appointment book was a brake rotation, because she was running on autopilot.

The hundred bucks she made on the job helped a little.

Every little bit she could sock away helped, because she had a surprise she was trying damn hard to pull off for Rosalie.

Their families may not understand each other. The wedding planner might be a nightmare. They may have had their first venue back out on them. And they might be pulling this whole wedding together on a shoestring.

But damn it, Sage was going to take Rosalie on the honeymoon of her dreams.

CARA MALONE

Rosalie was sacrificing a lot to humor Sage's mother and Stella. She was bending over backward to make the whole process as low-stress as it could be for Sage. She thought they weren't going to be able to afford a real honeymoon and she said they'd find something nice to do locally – make a weekend trip, it'd be nice as long as they did it together.

And she was right, it would be nice. But she deserved the world, and Sage was determined to give her this one thing.

A once-in-a-lifetime trip to the Netherlands at the height of the Aurora Borealis viewing season, with time to explore the region Rosalie's family was from along with all the other beautiful things the country had to offer.

Sage had been planning it for a few weeks now, gathering information and plotting out how to make it all happen. Rosalie was going to be knocked off her socks when Sage finally told her... but first she had to make sure they could afford it. And it was going to be a hell of an expensive trip.

She was taking on as many clients as she could fit into her appointment book, working double the hours she usually did, and the muscle twitches caused by her medications made it frustrating at times, but it was all temporary.

Worth it.

Her brake job came in to pick up his vehicle and handed her two wrinkly fifty-dollar bills, and Sage's stomach growled angrily as she pulled his car out of the bay. She'd gotten a late start this morning thanks to a certain furry someone who'd buried her housekeys in the couch, and all she'd had time for as she ran out the door was a protein bar.

Now it was two in the afternoon and she'd worked through lunch.

"Thanks a lot," her client said as she stepped out of the car and he slid behind the wheel. "You always do a nice job."

"Tell your friends that, okay?" she said, passing him a business card with her number on it.

Eating takeout wasn't going to get her and Rosalie any closer to the Netherlands, but she was suddenly so hungry she was starting to feel lightheaded. She could go home and make a sandwich, but that was at least half an hour roundtrip, not including the attention Bear would need if she showed her face in the apartment, and her next appointment was in fifteen minutes.

If her mother knew how hard she was working and how little she was paying attention to her body...

But this was for Rosalie, and it was important.

Sage went back inside the garage, heading in the direction of the break room. There was a vending machine there and a Snickers and a soda would only set her back three bucks and a couple minutes.

"Yo, Evans," somebody called as she walked through the garage.

She looked to the bay next to hers, where the owner, Henry, worked. He was currently on his back on a creeper, about to roll under a pick-up in need of an oil change.

"What's up?" Sage called back.

"You got time this afternoon?"

Sage frowned. She really didn't, and she'd promised Rosalie that she'd be home in time to take Bear out for his evening walk because Rosalie had an interview for her column tonight.

"Client just called," Henry went on. "Battery died, they're having the car towed here and they just need it swapped out, but I can't do it, I'm all booked up."

It was an easy job, and theoretically a fast one too, as long as nothing was corroded and the right part was available. Plus, it was always good to be useful around the shop – get a reputation for doing favors and soon people were doing them for you, too.

Sage was fully booked as well, but...

"When do you expect them?" she asked.

"Any minute," Henry said. "They don't need it till seven, though, so you can fit them in whenever." Maybe he could see her hesitation because he added, "It's a Merc and she's a good tipper."

Sage pressed her lips together, knowing she was about to do the wrong thing. "Yeah, let me know when the car arrives."

She went into the break room, slammed a Snickers and downed half a Mountain Dew in a single chug, then got back to work, the caffeine buzzing its way through her veins.

25

ROSALIE

The apartment was still dark when Rosalie got home about two hours later than usual. Unexpected, but maybe Sage took Bear for a walk and they weren't back yet. She'd just go collapse on the couch and wait for them, and then they'd figure out dinner–

On her first step inside the door, she kicked off her shoes in their usual place. And on her second step, her sock became wet.

"Oh fuck," she grumbled, peeling the dog-pee-soaked sock off. "Bear?"

He came trotting into the kitchen, looking guilty for the puddle but equally happy to see her.

"Where's Sage?" Rosalie asked him. "Didn't she come home and walk you?"

It was a rhetorical question – he couldn't fetch worth a damn and he didn't understand the meaning of the word 'stay,' but Rosalie could count on one hand the number of accidents he'd had in the apartment. None of them were his fault. She and Sage had gotten caught in traffic, or had work meetings run late, and once when they first got him, they simply forgot they were responsible for another creature's bladder and impulsively went out to dinner after work.

Rosalie dropped her wet sock in the sink – she'd deal with that later – and grabbed Bear's leash from the hook by the door. "Come on, let's go outside."

She walked him barefoot through the grass in front of the apartment, and while Bear gratefully did his business, Rosalie dialed Sage's number.

She got her voicemail and left a message.

"Babe, I thought you were going to walk Bear tonight. I had that interview with the EMT, remember? It went really well – I got a lot of good material for my column. Anyway, I hope you just got held up at work or something... love you."

She was trying not to worry, but it was pretty unlike Sage to drop the ball like this. Usually she'd at least text if something came up.

There was a voicemail from Stella, which Rosalie had noticed after her interview but hadn't had the energy to listen to yet. A missed call from Casey with no message, which generally just meant she was bored or had gossip. But nothing from Sage.

"Your mom's fine, she didn't forget about you," Rosalie told Bear as they headed back inside. "She's just... busy or something."

She cleaned up the puddle in the kitchen, rinsed her dirty sock, and called Casey back to kill the time. She had

Casey on speakerphone and was playing tug-of-war with Bear about half an hour later when the apartment door finally opened.

"I kept trying to tell her that I don't think you two are feathers-and-crystals-as-centerpieces people," Casey was saying, "but–"

"Case, I gotta go, sorry!" Rosalie said, dashing into the kitchen.

Sage was unzipping her coveralls, looking worn down, her shoulders sloped.

"Babe, are you okay?" Rosalie asked.

"I'm sorry I'm late," Sage said. "I took an extra job as a favor, and you'd think changing out the battery on a luxury car would be easy, but–"

A surprising little flash of anger shot through Rosalie's belly. "You were just working?"

"Well, yeah..."

"Bear had an accident," she said. "And I stepped in it, and I spent the last hour trying not to worry that something bad happened to you because you're *never* late, and you didn't even call me back!"

The alarm in Sage's eyes told Rosalie that she was yelling, but she couldn't stop herself now that she'd gotten started.

"You're working so much lately that I feel like I barely ever see you, except for when we have to go meet Stella about some stupid idea she's had – she called me, by the way, I don't even want to know *what* that's about." The words streamed out of her, four months' worth of stress all bubbling to the surface at once. "And that paramedic I met with tonight? She had some really *horrifying* things to say about how poorly prepared EMTs and cops are to respond to mental health emergencies. She told me about this incident at a bus stop..."

The paramedic had told the story in such vivid detail that Rosalie actually felt like she was there. Rosalie was planning to include the story in her article verbatim.

"A man was having a psychotic episode and he got off the bus completely disoriented," she continued. "He had no ID on him and he had no idea where he was. He couldn't tell the EMTs who to contact, so he ended up being put on a seventy-two-hour hold, all alone, until he was finally able to give an emergency contact. I just..."

"You were thinking about me in that situation," Sage said softly.

"I know you're doing well and your symptoms are managed, but I had all that running through my head while I was wondering where you were—"

"Rosalie!" Sage put her hands on her shoulders, disrupting the stream of worries exploding out of her. Rosalie quieted, and Sage pulled her into her arms. "I'm fine. I'm so sorry I worried you."

Rosalie sank against her. "I'd worry about you no matter what because I love you, but it wasn't until I started writing this column that I realized just how fucked up and broken our mental health services are."

"They are," Sage agreed, holding her tighter. "But you're doing something to fix it by raising awareness, and I'm fine. I can't promise I'm going to be fine every day for the rest of our lives... in fact, I won't be. But neither will you, with or without mental illness. I *can* promise to keep my phone ringer on so I notice when you call me, and to let you know if I'm going to be running late. Okay?"

"Okay." Rosalie drew Sage into a kiss, gentle at first and increasingly needy. Her mouth opened and their tongues entwined, hands grabbing each other with urgency.

"Don't forget to apologize to Bear too!" The voice was tinny and distant, and for a second, Rosalie was extremely confused.

"Oh shit," she laughed. "Casey's still on speakerphone."

"Yeah, take me off it before I hear something we all regret," she said. "I know what that sudden silence means."

"Goodnight, Casey," Sage laughed as Rosalie crossed the room to hang up the phone. When she returned, Sage asked, "Are we all right?"

"Of course," Rosalie said, kissing her again. "Casey's right, though. Bear would appreciate a bacon-flavored apology."

Bear's ears instantly perked up at the B-word and Sage went into the kitchen to retrieve a doggy ice cream cup from the freezer. She set it down and Bear pounced, lapping it up enthusiastically.

"Well, he's occupied for the next twenty minutes. What should we do?"

"I can think of one thing, but it might take longer than twenty minutes," Rosalie winked. Then she put her hand on her rumbling stomach. "On the other hand, I'm famished."

"It's way past dinner, and I had a candy bar for lunch," Sage said.

"Babe!"

"I was swamped. It was the best I could do."

Rosalie shook her head disapprovingly. "I'm going to have to start packing you a lunch in the mornings. Gotta make sure my baby eats right, takes care of herself."

"Thanks, Mom," Sage teased, but she kissed the top of Rosalie's head, then started listing off the takeout options that they preferred. "What are you in the mood for?"

"Let's just get a pizza," Rosalie said. "I need a lot of food and fast." She picked up her phone to order, then rolled her eyes. "And while we wait, we should find out what Stella wants."

"Ugh, do we have to?"

Rosalie placed the order – their usual, half pepperoni and mushroom, half sausage, with cinnamon breadsticks for dessert – then dragged Sage over to the couch to listen to Stella's voicemail.

"Hi, girl!" her chipper voice filled the apartment as soon as Rosalie hit play. "I wanted to give you an update on the centerpieces I'm working on with Casey – they're *gorgeous.*"

"Feathery, apparently," Rosalie said to Sage, whose eyes went wide.

"And the new venue sent back all the paperwork, everything's approved so that's good."

"For twice what the first venue cost," Sage added.

"And the wedding invitations have arrived from the printer," Stella said, and even on the recording, Rosalie could hear the strain in her voice. Here it came... "There was just one small problem."

"Fuuu..." Sage groaned theatrically.

"I accidentally approved the wrong proof when I was doing the ordering and the printer used the Grand Chateau template instead of the Elegant Simplicity one you chose."

"Grand Chateau... that's the one with all the glitter and gold embossing, isn't it?" Sage asked.

Rosalie nodded, rolling her eyes. "The one Stella loved."

"I took a picture of what came in," Stella continued on the voicemail. "I emailed it to you both to take a look. If you hate it, we absolutely have time to re-order the invites... but since it was my error, the printing company won't reimburse us for the cost... and at this point there'll need to be a rush printing charge added." Her voice regained its chipperness. "Let me know what you think, look forward to hearing from you! So exciting, we're getting so close!"

The voicemail ended, and Rosalie switched over to her email app. She found the message from Stella and clicked on the attachment, turning the screen toward Sage.

"Yeah, that's the wrong design, all right," she sighed.

"I mean, neither of us would have chosen this, but it's just the invite," Rosalie shrugged. "Can we really justify the expense of having them reprinted at this point?"

Sage squinted at the screen, then took the phone out of Rosalie's hand to examine the picture closer. "*The pleasure of your company is requested to celebrate the marriage of Rosalie West and Ssage Evans,*" she read, drawing out the S. "She misspelled my name."

"You gotta be fucking kidding me." Rosalie snatched the phone back, enlarging the image. Yup, right there in garish gold glitter – S*sage*. "Well, I guess we're re-ordering."

"Wait," Sage said. "I have another solution. How do you feel about being married to someone who's got their tongue split? I could lean into it, sstart drawing out all my Ss. You like ssnakes, right, babe?"

Rosalie had been on the verge of spiking her phone into the coffee table, frustrated to tears at yet another setback in the wedding from hell. But now she had tears in her eyes for another reason, doubling over with laughter.

"Oh my god, do *not* split your tongue."

"But imagine what I could do with it," Sage said, wiggling her brows.

The thought actually did make Rosalie's cheeks heat up, but she shook her head. "I think we can find less permanent ways to spice things up in the bedroom."

"You mean sspice them up?" Sage was getting in her face and making goofy expressions every time she hissed an S-word, and Rosalie was starting to get a stitch in her side.

"Stop," she whined. "How can you do that?"

"What?"

"Make everything instantly better, no matter how much it sucks."

"I'm just sspecial, I guess."

Rosalie pounced on her, kissing her ferociously until Sage was no longer capable of hissing or teasing or anything but returning her affections. So the wedding invitations were the wrong design, and one of the brides' names wasn't even spelled right. So they'd be getting married in fancy clothing in an event hall far grander than anything they'd ever wanted for themselves.

The only really important thing was the two of them.

It was *their* wedding, so it would be perfect.

A perfect trainwreck, maybe, but perfect nonethelessss.

26

SAGE

"Are you sure you're taking care of yourself?" Sage's mom asked, frowning at her from across the bistro table.

The two of them were sitting on the patio outside one of the best breakfast spots in the area. It was walking distance from the apartment, and Bear was welcome in the outdoor area – he was lying on top of Sage's feet, enthusiastically licking the whipped cream from a tiny cup. They'd been here all of five minutes, and already Sage felt like her mother was attempting to look into her soul.

"I'm fine," she said, trying and failing to keep the defensiveness from her tone. It came out whenever her mom got all smothery. "Just tired."

"Willow says you're working a lot more than usual."

"Well, the wedding is expensive. Especially with our wedding planner." She couldn't resist that last remark, and her mom frowned again.

"Are you still clashing with her?"

Sage laughed. "I wouldn't call it clashing exactly. More like bashing our heads against a brick wall named Stella."

Her mom laughed. "She *is* hard-headed. You should have seen her reaction at work when we switched from that ancient timeclock to the new scheduling software. You'd have thought they were asking her to do rocket science every time she clocks in."

"She's not good with technology?" That surprised Sage, because Stella loved Facetime and she was always sending emails at three in the morning when she saw a fun new idea for a sundae bar or a photobooth on Pinterest.

"She's just not good with change. Anyway," her mom smiled. "Tell me about your new garage. The boss isn't keeping you *too* busy, is he?"

This was her way of turning the conversation back to the topic of whether Sage was taking care of herself. After twenty-nine years with the woman, her machinations were more transparent than she liked to think, and Sage knew exactly what she was really asking.

"Henry's not my boss, he just rents the stall to me. I set my own schedule," she assured her mom. "I only take as many clients as I want to." And whoever Henry sent her way, although she didn't mention that. "Plus it's really convenient – right down the street."

"Well, you look like you could use more sleep."

Sage rolled her eyes. "Gee, thanks."

"I'm sorry, I don't say that to be mean, but you have

dark circles under your eyes," her mom insisted. "When you lived at home, you worked about four hours a day – and you had a lot less stress in general."

Read: you're not strong enough to push yourself this hard.

Sage tightened her grip on the mug in her hand. "I'm perfectly capable of managing my stress. Just because I have schizophrenia doesn't mean I have to be dependent on you for the rest of my life."

She narrowly bit back a further comment about how her mother would probably love it if she moved back home and allowed her to baby her for the rest of her life. Sometimes it sure felt like that was what she was angling for.

Her mom reached across the table, taking her hand. "You're right, and I know that. It's just that I'm your mother and it's my job to worry about you. It's not just you – I worry about Willow too."

Sage snorted. "I know, she had an actual counter on her phone for how many times you asked her about her gestational diabetes when she was pregnant with Tommy."

Her mom's cheeks colored. "Do I want to know the number?"

"It was in the triple digits."

"Yikes." She took a sip of her own coffee, then cleared her throat. "Anyway, let's talk about something else. Have you heard she's planning to homeschool Robbie?"

Sage laughed. She *had* heard about that, and maybe it was just big sister syndrome, but she couldn't for the life of her imagine Willow playing the schoolteacher role. Especially not with her firstborn, who got whatever he wanted with the bat of an eyelash.

"He's going to spend all his time studying dinosaurs," she said. "He'll have a doctorate on stegosauruses but he won't be able to write his name."

"Your sister isn't *that* much of a doormat," her mom said, but the glimmer in her eyes said otherwise.

As they hypothesized what Willow the Teacher would look like, a thought nagged at the back of Sage's mind in her mother's voice. Did she skip a dose of her meds? She took them last night... she must have, because she took them every night right after she brushed her teeth for bed.

Although last night, she and Rosalie made love right after they finished eating dinner, and then fell asleep for a while... Sage woke up around two a.m. to Bear complaining that he never got his bedtime potty break and she'd taken him out in her PJs.

And the night before, she'd been so wiped out from a full day of rapid-fire oil changes that she fell asleep on the couch watching old episodes of *Rizzoli & Isles.* Rosalie had woken her up and drug her to bed.

Shit. Did she skip two days of meds? She'd be feeling it soon if so.

As soon as she got home, she'd take a dose, even if it knocked her out at seven p.m.

"Honey?"

"Hmm?"

"You zoned out." Her mom was frowning again, no

doubt back to worrying about her, reading far too much into Sage's every move.

"Sorry – like I said, tired." She took a long sip of her coffee. "Two more months to the wedding, and then everything goes back to normal."

Her mom's eyes lit up. "Oh! I can't believe I forgot to mention it till now, we got our invite." She picked her purse up off the ground and riffled through it, pulling out a wedding invite in a deep crimson envelope. "I thought you two decided on a cream and soft green color palette."

"Yes, we did," Sage grumbled. She took the invite – the first one she'd actually seen in person. The design wasn't the worst thing in the world. It had the date of the wedding, and the address of the venue... that was all that was really important, right? She laughed and pointed to her name. "Did you see my other news? I've decided to go by Ssage from now on."

Her mom winced. "I did see that, I wasn't going to mention it. Stella's handiwork again?"

"Who else?"

Sage handed the invite back, and her mom tucked it in her purse, which Bear immediately assumed was a game of hide-and-seek and he started snuffling around.

"Honey, I'm sorry I set you up with her," Sage's mom said. "I really was trying to help, take something off your plate. I had no idea she was going to make the whole thing *more* difficult for you two."

"I know you were." Sage let out a long sigh, then laughed. "She's driving us literally insane. I think I noticed a bald spot on the back of Rosalie's head the other day."

"If it's any consolation, Stella is stressing herself out just as much as you two. She was crying – no, sobbing – at her desk the day your first venue cancelled and our boss had to send her on her break before she scared away any customers."

Sage weighed whether that actually was a consolation. Better than if Stella didn't care at all about the myriad fuck-ups she'd made, but still...

"It'd be so much easier to deal with her if it was just a bunch of well-meaning mistakes," she said. "But it's like she's planning *her* dream wedding instead of ours. She doesn't listen to us at all."

"She's just excited–"

"She's just a maniac."

"–and it's her first wedding–"

Sage's jaw dropped. "Umm, what?"

Her mom's eyes rounded as she realized what she'd said.

"Mom!"

"Okay, she's never planned a wedding before!" she confessed. "But she's been working on her business for over a year – she's *always* talking about it to anyone at work who will listen, and she's got binders upon binders of ideas. I thought she just needed someone to give her a chance, and you needed some help... it seemed like the perfect pairing."

Sage rubbed her temple. "You made Rosalie and me be Stella's guinea pigs."

"If I'd known..."

"Didn't you think there was some reason she'd never gotten any clients for over a year?"

"I thought she needed a confidence boost. I just wanted to help."

Sage let out a long breath. The outrage that had risen to the surface dissipated a bit. "Yeah, I know you did. You always just want to help everyone, and I love you for it."

"You're not mad?"

"No. But I am *not* writing Stella a positive Yelp review when this is all over."

"I wouldn't ask you to."

"And you better not either," Sage warned. "I wouldn't wish her on some other unsuspecting couple."

"Are you going to fire her?" Her mom winced again. "I shouldn't be telling you this, but our boss is not a big fan of her and our performance reviews are coming up soon. I think she's too sensitive to handle getting fired from two jobs right now."

Sage sighed. "No, I will not fire her. The wedding is basically planned at this point – I don't know how much more damage she could do." She lifted her coffee cup, then said, "But people are stronger than you give them credit for, Mom. I am, and I bet Stella is too." She took a sip, then added with a smirk, "Bear is chewing on a panty liner from your purse."

"Oh my god," her mom said, snatching it up and stuffing it back in her bag.

27

ROSALIE

osalie could smell the greasy, heavenly aroma of Giovanni's Pizza before they even got to Casey's apartment door. It was an old favorite of theirs growing up, a neighborhood staple, and Rosalie had taken great joy in introducing it to Sage. Now she loved it just as much as they did.

"Are you literally drooling?" Sage teased as she glanced sidelong at Rosalie.

"No," she said defensively, swiping at the corner of her mouth and then giving Sage a wink.

Sage smiled, then her phone dinged in her pocket and she whipped it out, texting a reply.

"Anything important?" Rosalie asked. Sage had been texting during the car ride over too.

"Just work," she mumbled. "Sorry."

The door opened, and Casey stood before them with a bottle of beer already in hand. That was an addition to their old high school Friday night rituals, added once they were old enough to drink. Rosalie usually passed, but she couldn't deny a cold beer and a hot slice were a winning combination.

Casey, though, looked like this wasn't her first of the night.

"You okay?" Rosalie asked as Casey stepped aside.

"Been better," she said. "Come on in and I'll tell you about it."

They didn't get pizza every Friday night anymore – life was too hectic for that – but Rosalie always looked forward to it, all the more since Casey and Sage had begun to bond too.

Inside the apartment, the familiar white and red pizza box waited on the kitchen table, along with a fat stack of napkins, a bowl of chips and the rest of the six-pack. As Rosalie suspected, there were only three left.

"So, what's up?" Rosalie asked gently as they all took their usual seats at the table.

"That guy I was seeing," Casey said, flopping into her chair, "Jay?"

"Yeah?"

Casey grabbed a fistful of chips from the bowl and stuffed them all in her cheeks at once. Little bits of potato flew across the table as she said, "He was sleeping with other women the whole entire time we were dating!"

"Seriously? What a dick!"

Rosalie was genuinely pissed, but she was also trying to remember how long Casey and Jay had dated. A best friend should know that, but Casey didn't have the best luck with men and it was sometimes hard to keep track of them.

"I mean, good riddance," Casey grumbled. "If he can't even be exclusive for three months, I can only imagine what a long-term relationship would have been like." She pouted and reached for her beer. "But he was so cute."

Rosalie gave her a teasing grin. "If you say so."

"I know, not your type." Casey flipped open the pizza box and she and Rosalie dug in. Sage answered another notification from her phone. "Hey, maybe I should try your type. Your love life was a trainwreck before you switched to girls, maybe it could work for me too."

Rosalie laughed. "You never know until you try. Sage knows some single queer women from the hot shop if you want an introduction."

They both looked at Sage, who still had her nose in her phone.

Rosalie nudged her with her elbow. "Babe?"

"Hmm? Oh, men suck," Sage said, oblivious to the fact that she was about five minutes late on that comment.

"Are you okay?" Rosalie asked.

Finally, Sage put down her phone, looking at the two of them like she just realized she wasn't curled up on the couch at home. "I'm sorry. Henry's got a complicated engine repair he wants me to help with – I was just coor-dinating schedules with him, but it can wait."

She turned her phone ringer off and tucked the device in her breast pocket.

"Are you sure?" Rosalie asked. "I don't want you to miss out on a job."

"It's fine, I'll see him tomorrow," Sage said, then reached for a slice of pizza. "Anyway... yes, I can introduce you to some of my glassblowing friends."

"Well," Casey blushed. "Let's hold off on that for now – I'm not sure I've recovered from Jay yet." She polished off her third beer with a grimace, then brightened. "Okay, moving on from my sordid affairs... tell me about wedding planning. Any more Stella gossip?"

"Oh my god, please don't even say that name," Sage groaned. "Did you get your invite in the mail yet?"

Casey cackled. "Yesssss, I did. It's beautiful."

"They're tacky," Rosalie said, "but what's done is done."

"So are the centerpieces we worked on. I'll show them to you once we're done eating," Casey said. "So, are we going to burn Stella in effigy once this whole thing is over or what?"

"I promised my mother I'd be nice to her," Sage said. "However, I do have some disturbing news to share... which may not be all that surprising."

Rosalie's eyebrows rose. "You didn't tell me you had news."

"It sslipped my mind," Sage answered. "When I got breakfast with my mom the other day, she said Stella has never had a client before us."

Casey burst into laughter again. She wasn't quite drunk, but she was well on her way to tipsy and enjoying herself thoroughly. That was fine, a welcome change from how sullen she looked when she answered the door.

"You better eat that," Rosalie said, nodding to the pizza on Casey's plate. Then she turned to her fiancée. "You're right, I'm not in the least bit surprised, but what was your mom thinking when she hired her?"

"What she always is," Sage sighed. "That Stella was a baby bird who fell out of the nest, and she needed my mom's help."

"Aww," Casey fawned. "Your mom is sweet."

"Overbearing," Sage corrected.

"That too," Casey laughed.

Rosalie wisely chose to remain silent on the subject of her future mother-in-law's personality flaws.

They moved on to other topics – work, more pleasant aspects of the wedding planning, whether Rosalie would look good with cotton-candy-pink hair, what Casey's type might be if she did date women. The pizza disappeared quickly, along with most of the bowl of chips, and Sage and Casey both had beer.

Rosalie thought about joining them. Things *had* been stressful lately, and a little buzz would feel nice and help her wind down. Lots of people did that at the end of the week.

But those people may or may not have addict parents, and she always felt a pang of concern when she caught herself thinking things like that.

So she drank soda, enjoyed her pizza just as much, and when the box was empty but for the grease stains, the three of them got up and headed for the living room couch to keep chatting.

"Should we clean up first?" Rosalie offered.

"Leave it, the butler will get it," Casey snorted. That latest beer had tipped her over into drunk, but she was having fun and not wallowing about Jay. At least she wasn't the type to get angry when she drank.

"We'll put the plates in the dishwasher before we leave," Rosalie promised as she sat down on the couch.

Casey plopped down on a big, cozy armchair surrounded with candles and books, and flicked on a table lamp. Sage had frozen halfway between the kitchen and the living room, her phone in her hand again.

"Babe?" Rosalie prompted.

Sage was frowning, and a pit formed in Rosalie's stomach. She wasn't usually like this, glued to her phone, disconnected from the people around her. Something was up.

"I'm really sorry but I just need to make a quick call," Sage said before disappearing out the front door.

Okay, that was *really* not like her. Why did she have to go all the way outside for that? Just to talk to Henry about car stuff?

"Umm, what's up with her?" Casey asked.

Rosalie pinched the bridge of her nose, trying to fend off a tension headache. "I don't know."

There was no reason Sage couldn't have made a work call from the kitchen. She'd done stuff like that before, so what was different now? Was she even really talking to Henry?

"You think she's cheating on you?" Casey blurted it out, more blunt thanks to the beer.

"Oh my god, no," Rosalie said.

"Jay was always secretive with his phone."

"She's not cheating," Rosalie said. The thought had honestly never crossed her mind – Sage wouldn't do that. "I am worried, though."

"She's acting weird, right?" Casey agreed.

Rosalie nodded, thinking.

Casey knew Sage had schizophrenia. Sage had told her a couple months after they all started hanging out together, once she felt comfortable with Casey. Letting people know helped explain some of her symptoms – like when it took her a little longer than other people to gather her thoughts, or when her medications gave her muscle spasms. But they'd never really talked about it in depth, and Rosalie didn't feel right talking about it with Casey when Sage wasn't present.

"She's going to be your wife," Casey said, getting riled up again. "If she's hiding something from you, you have a right to know what it is. Secrets kill relationships."

Rosalie folded her arms over her chest. Whatever the problem was, Sage was clearly keeping something from her. But it wasn't what Casey was thinking.

"We've had so much stress these last few months with all the wedding planning, all the fuck-ups," she vented. "And she's working more than usual – like, a *lot* more. I keep telling her she doesn't have to pay for this wedding all by herself, we could have a courthouse wedding and

I'd be happy. I'm worried she's piling too much on herself."

"What do you mean?"

"I'm worried about her mental health." Rosalie had never seen Sage in the middle of a psychotic episode, but they'd talked a lot about what those episodes had been like for Sage in the past, and what Rosalie might notice if something was going wrong with Sage's medications or therapy.

Being secretive, paranoid, acting cagey? That was definitely part of it. And stress could bring symptoms on. Plus, she wasn't even going to her weekly group therapy sessions right now. She still saw Dr. Khan once a month, but she said group was eating into her schedule too much, and she'd start going again after the wedding.

"Isn't she on meds?" Casey asked.

"Yes, but they're not perfect," Rosalie said. "She still has breakthrough symptoms from time to time. They're mostly minor, auditory hallucinations that she can identify and ignore, brain fog, stuff like that. But what if they're getting worse and she's not telling me because she doesn't want to worry me?"

Now, *that* was a familiar scenario. How many times had she asked her father, point blank, if he was drinking again, only for him to tell her no? And then later, when she found the empties or smelled the alcohol on his breath, he'd say he just didn't want to burden her.

"That's really scary. It hasn't happened since you started dating her. How do you even know you could handle it?"

Rosalie's brow furrowed. "How does Sage handle it? I'm sure it sucks but she has no choice – she gets through it, and so would I."

Casey bit her bottom lip, then shrugged. "I mean, you don't *have* to handle it."

"What's that supposed to mean?"

"You're not married yet."

"What's that supposed to mean?" Rosalie asked.

"I just think you have rose-colored glasses about this whole situation," Casey insisted, seeming to have sobered up in the last few minutes. "You're in love, the new-relationship endorphins are flowing, you're not thinking about what it could be like, long-term, to live with someone who has such a serious mental illness."

"I'm not thinking about it? I've spent the last six months educating myself and everyone who reads the Gazette about mental health issues. And what have you done to learn more about your best friend's fiancée's condition? Watched a couple YouTube videos after *I* asked you to."

"Oh, so now it's my fault?" Casey stood up.

"This ridiculous, insensitive conversation is your fault," Rosalie pointed out. "And if you still want to even be in the wedding, I think you better–"

Before Rosalie could finish her sentence, the front door opened and Sage reappeared looking slightly red in the face. She froze near the door, looking back and forth between the two of them.

"Did I just walk in on a fight?"

Casey looked to Rosalie, who was sitting with her

arms crossed over her chest. She uncrossed them and tried to smile reassuringly. The last thing she wanted was for Sage to find out any of what Casey just said.

"Nope, we're good," she said.

"I was just getting another beer. Want one?" Casey asked. "I have more in the fridge."

"No thanks."

Casey went into the kitchen and Rosalie asked, "Everything okay with your call?"

"Yeah, sorry about that," Sage said. "Good news, though, while I was on the phone I walked down to the corner store and got us dessert."

She upended a paper grocery bag on the coffee table and a variety of Hostess snacks rained down. Rosalie grabbed a cherry Fruit Pie – nothing but sugar masquerading as fruit, wrapped in more sugar pretending to be pie crust, but delicious as hell. She packed her anger at Casey away, in the same part of her mind where she stored up her worries about Sage.

Not tonight. Not until after the wedding, if possible.

Sage sank down beside her with a pack of Cupcakes, wrapping her arm comfortingly around Rosalie's shoulder. On her way back to her chair, Casey snagged a HoHo, saying, "They should rename these JayJays. Cuz he's a ho."

Okay, maybe she wasn't *entirely* sober again yet.

2 8

SAGE

"I'm just worried about you, that's all," Rosalie said as she hopped down from the passenger side of Sage's truck, Bear already on the sidewalk waiting impatiently for her.

Sage bristled, but tried not to show it. "I'm fine."

She'd been saying this all week, and she was getting tired of reassuring everyone. It started with her mom and that coffee date, and then Rosalie got the wrong idea on pizza night with Casey, but Sage couldn't tell her the real reason she'd been so distracted.

One of the mechanics at the garage knew a guy who knew a guy who was really good at finding vacation deals, and she'd been playing phone tag with him all week, trying to make their dream honeymoon a reality. They were only a month out from the wedding, and when he finally called her back, she couldn't just let it go to voicemail.

So she *was* acting sketchy, but not for the reason

everyone thought. And she was trying not to get irritated by the fact that everyone in her life seemed to think she was one stressful event away from the psych ward.

Even Rosalie...

She'd never seen Sage at her worst, and Sage had worked very hard to keep it that way. And she *still* wound up hovering, fussing, mothering.

"I just—"

"Please," Sage cut her off as she came around the truck and took her hand. "We're about to walk into our bridal shower and both our families are in there. For once, Stella *isn't* going to be here. I just want to enjoy the evening, and I want you to believe me when I tell you that any stress I'm feeling is just the usual wedding planning anxiety. Everything is going to be fine. I love you."

Rosalie threw her arms around Sage's waist, nestling into her. "I love you too. I'm sorry."

"Me too. I haven't been at a hundred percent lately."

"Neither of us has," Rosalie said, then laughed. "Who knew getting married would be the hardest thing we ever did?"

"Can you imagine when we're ready to start having kids?" Sage snorted. "God, I hope Stella hasn't decided to be a doula by then."

"We'd have no choice but to flee the state."

"The country."

"I hear it's lovely on the moon."

They kissed, then stepped through the front door. They were at Sage's parents' house, which had a big back yard well-suited for entertaining. Sage's mom had planned the whole thing and all they had to do was show up – so far, it was the smoothest any of their wedding events had gone.

"Here they are, the women of honor!" Angela said the minute they crossed the threshold.

"Wait, I thought I was the maid of honor," Willow teased from the snack table where she was setting out veggies and dip.

"One of them," Casey shot back as she ushered Rosalie, Sage and Bear in. Rosalie seemed to bristle at her nearness, but maybe Sage was just misreading their body language. "People are starting to arrive, and we've been sending them out back since it's nice out."

"Your dad's firing up the grill now, so we'll eat in about an hour," Sage's mom said, coming into the room with a tray full of cocktail meatballs. "Unless you need something now?"

"We can wait sixty minutes, Mom."

"Thanks, Mrs. Evans," Rosalie said, nodding in agreement.

"Call me Angela if you won't call me Mom," she said. It wasn't the first time she'd made the request, but Rosalie just gave a polite chuckle, then steered Sage and Bear toward the back yard.

"Not ready to adopt my mom?" Sage asked as they walked through the kitchen.

Rosalie shrugged. "It just feels a little weird. Would you want to call my dad Pop?"

"He hasn't asked me to," Sage pointed out. "I barely know him."

"Well, he didn't want to come today," Rosalie said bitterly. "Even though your dad will be here, it's not like this is a girls-only event. Anyway..." She huffed, then kissed Sage's temple. "Let's mingle."

The back yard held about half a dozen people, including Sage's grandma and several people who looked like they were from Rosalie's family tree, judging by the wavy blonde hair.

There was a drinks table set up on the patio, and soft instrumental music was playing over outdoor speakers that Sage and her dad had installed years ago. The yard smelled freshly mown, and it was a warm, sunny spring day.

It should have been serene, comforting.

But an unsettled feeling was gnawing inside Sage's stomach. It started with Rosalie asking her for the hundredth time if she was okay, and now she couldn't help wondering if there was more to the fact that Rosalie didn't want to call Angela Mom.

Did she *really* want to be a part of Sage's family?

What if she changed her mind?

"Wow, look at all the drink options," Rosalie pointed out. "Your mom really outdid herself."

Sage pushed the thought aside and turned her attention to the party. There were dispensers filled with lemonade, fresh fruit bobbing on top. Sparkling waters with fruity syrups to mix and match as you pleased. A galvanized tub filled with ice and every microbrew Hickory Harbor had to offer.

"What's your poison?" Sage asked, grabbing a stemless wineglass from a row of them on the table.

"Lemonade, I guess."

While Sage filled Rosalie's glass, she saw Casey step onto the patio. Rosalie looked at her, then turned back to Sage. Weird, and she hadn't greeted her best friend too warmly when they first arrived, either.

"Are you two fighting or something?" Sage asked as she handed over the glass then looked through the tub of microbrews.

"No." Rosalie's answer was clipped, and she immediately took a sip of her drink. "Ooh, this is good."

"You two haven't been in a fight since I met you," Sage pointed out. It sure seemed like they were fighting now. "Did something happen?"

"Now who's nagging?" Rosalie asked with a smile. "Come on, let's go make the rounds, greet our guests."

Sage snagged a blonde ale from the tub and popped the cap, then followed Rosalie and Bear into the fray. Casey stayed on the other side of the party for a few minutes, tried and failed to catch Rosalie's eye a couple times, then disappeared back inside.

There was definitely something wrong there, but Sage didn't have the mental space to figure it out right now. The next half an hour was a whirlwind of new names and faces, and distant relatives that Sage hadn't seen in ages. Her heart leapt into her throat every single time someone approached them because there was always the possibility that her brain would choose that exact moment to stop working. *This is my aunt...* and then a total blank. And then it would feel like everyone at the party was staring at her and thinking, *You've known her your whole life and she sends you twenty dollars and a card for every birthday, but you can't remember her name, you ungrateful jerk?*

Thankfully, Sage always managed to spit out the proper name just in time, and no one ever seemed to notice the panicked struggle going on behind her words.

Now, was she going to remember the names of any of Rosalie's extended family members after today? Making it extremely awkward when they all remembered her name at the wedding?

Yeah, that would be fun...

When Sage saw her dad coming through the sliding door from the kitchen with a big tray piled high with kebabs, she saw an escape route.

"I'm gonna go see if Dad needs any help," she said, kissing Rosalie and leaving her with her Aunt Kathy.

Rosalie gave her a little frown, but let her go – she was probably the only one there who could see the need for a break etched into Sage's features. "Have fun, babe."

"Hey, kiddo," her dad said as she and Bear approached the grill. "How you doing?"

"Not bad, wanted to see if the grill master needs an assistant."

"The master needs no help," he said, then grinned. "But he'd love to spend a little time chatting with you. Want to start laying kebabs?"

He opened the grill and heat and smoke billowed out from the charcoal he must have lit before Sage and Rosalie arrived. It was perfectly piled up and ready to go.

"Sure."

Sage tethered Bear's leash to the patio railing a safe distance away and they worked silently for a minute or two, arranging skewers full of various marinated meats and veggies on the grill. Sage watched people filter in and out of the sliding door, and she could hear Rosalie regaling someone new with the ordeal of Stella, the World's Worst Wedding Planner.

She could also hear Casey near the drinks table, speaking softly to someone. Sage could only make out a word here and there... *fault... hands full... too much.*

Was she talking about Sage, saying she was too much for Rosalie?

When she turned her head to see who Casey was telling all this to, the refreshment table was unoccupied. She must have left already.

Sage turned back to the grill as her dad was closing it.

"Those will be ready in about ten minutes, I'd say." He looked at the beer she'd set on the railing. "What are you drinking?"

"A Vanilla Skies blonde ale," she said, picking it up again.

"Any good?"

"Yeah, wanna try?"

Her dad had a sip, then went over to the drinks table to get one for himself. When he returned to the grill, he put his arm around Sage's shoulder and they turned to look at the groups of people chatting around them. Rosalie looked over and smiled at Sage, and her dad said, "I'm proud of you, kid."

That pit in Sage's stomach gave a pang, reminding her that it was there. "For what?"

"Are you kidding me?" He gave her a sidelong look, then swept his arm at the scene before them. "You found yourself a great partner. You're doing better than ever with your business. You've found your rhythm and you're thriving. You have all these people who love and support you. What's not to be proud of?"

Sage felt her cheeks heating. "Thanks, Dad."

"I mean it," he pressed. "You should be proud of yourself too."

Some days, especially lately, it felt like everything was hanging by a thread and all Sage could do was pray it wouldn't break. And then there was the voice over her shoulder that said unhelpful things like, *Go get the scissors. Cut the thread. You don't deserve this, how could you think you did?*

"I am," she said weakly.

Her dad took his arm off her shoulder so he could face her. "You doing okay, kiddo?"

"Yes," Sage said with a little more conviction. "Everything's fine."

"Not working *too* hard?"

Oh boy, now he was starting in on her too...

"Remembering to take your meds? Go to bed at a reasonable hour?"

"Dad," she said sharply. "Can you please not do this? I already have Mom and Rosalie on my back. I'm fine."

He held up a hand in surrender. "Of course. We all just want you to know we're here for you."

"I know. I'm gonna go get one of those little meatballs."

"You can leave Bear with me," her dad said when she reached for his leash. "I'm sure he'd be thrilled if something were to *fall off* the grill."

Sage started to walk toward the sliding door. Willow was coming outside with Katie, and rather than wait for her niece to wobble her way over the threshold, Sage decided to keep walking.

"Hey, sis," Willow said as she passed.

"Hey," Sage nodded without stopping.

"Where are you going?"

"Just gonna take a minute."

Sage didn't actually know where she was going at first, but she stepped off the patio and once she was in the yard, the garage came into view around the side of the house. Her feet started to take her in that direction, and she found the door unlocked so she went inside.

It was dim and a little dusty, and her dad's car was parked in it now that Sage had moved out. The pegboards on the walls were all empty since she'd taken her tools with her, and the workbench was starting to fill up with odds and ends – junk from the house that her mother had probably asked her dad to store out here. Sage flipped open a cardboard box and found a set of steel cannoli forms that her great-grandmother had left to her mom. Her mom had never used them, but couldn't bring herself to throw them away.

"I can't even bake a cake, let alone something like

this," she'd complained way back when Gammy first mentioned wanting to pass them down.

"Well, maybe one of the girls will want them," Gammy had said, and Sage was only five at the time but she immediately shook her head.

"I don't bake."

"You'll learn," Gammy had insisted, and she'd willed a lot of her kitchen supplies to Angela. All these years later, there was still no one in the family brave enough to tackle the cannoli forms.

Sage pulled out her old stool from under the workbench and plopped down. A surprising plume of dust burst into the air. Had it really been that long since her life revolved around this garage?

There was a knock on the doorframe, then Willow popped her head inside. "Hey, can I come in?"

Sage nodded, pulling out the second stool with her foot. "Where's Katie?"

"Dad's teaching her the art of the grill." Willow sat down. "What are you doing in here? You're missing your party."

"I needed to breathe."

Willow laughed. "In here? It smells like motor oil and dust allergies."

"It's comforting."

Willow opened her mouth and Sage braced herself for yet another person asking her if she was okay. She physically tensed, and her little sister must have seen it because she didn't say anything after all. She just reached out and squeezed Sage's hand.

Then they sat in silence for a minute or two, until at last, Sage was the one to speak.

"It's just a lot."

"I know. I lost count of how many times I cried while Ron and I were planning our wedding."

"I lost count too," Sage teased. Then she gestured to the door. "Have they noticed I'm gone?"

"The usual suspects have," Willow told her. "And Rosalie just got cornered by Aunt Aggie, so I'm sure she'd love to see you."

"Okay, let's go." Sage slid off her stool. "Thanks for coming to check on me. And not nagging."

"Hey, I'm your little sister. I'm not supposed to nag you, I'm supposed to annoy the fuck out of you."

"Well, at this precise moment, you're doing neither and I really appreciate it."

They went back outside and Sage squinted. The sun seemed brighter after even a short time in the dim garage, and when she stepped back around the side of the house and spotted Rosalie, it made a halo effect around her blonde head. Sage grinned as she walked toward her fiancée.

"What?" Rosalie asked when she reached her.

"You're stunning," she said, kissing her and then turning to the group Rosalie was at the center of. "Aunt Aggie, how was your drive into town?"

"Horrendous," her aunt said with a dramatic sigh. "I was just telling Rosalie all about it, but your dad said we have a few more minutes until the food is ready so let me start over..."

181

29

ROSALIE

The bridal shower was... weird. Between the lingering resentment Rosalie was harboring about what Casey said on pizza night and her suspicion that something was up with Sage, there was a thick tension hanging over the whole thing.

They got through it, and even got a set of matching plates from the registry that they'd redone behind Stella's back. Rosalie hugged the box when she saw it, and put them in the cupboards right away when they got home.

"Are you happy?" Sage asked, watching her.

"About the plates?"

"Yes... and in general."

Rosalie stopped what she was doing to scoop Sage into a hug. "Babe, I'm happier than I've ever been before. I can't wait to be your wife."

Sage frowned. "But you're fighting with your best friend. Is it about me?"

Rosalie averted her eyes. "It's not about you," she fibbed.

"What's it about?"

"Umm, she's thinking about taking that cheater guy back," she blurted. "She doesn't want to go stag to the wedding and I don't want her to do that to herself."

None of that was true, and Rosalie couldn't think of another time that she'd lied to Sage. It didn't feel good, but telling her what Casey had actually said would feel worse.

Before Sage could ask any more questions, Rosalie exaggerated a yawn and said, "What do you think, is it bedtime?" Then she made a beeline for the bathroom.

Sage followed her and they shared the sink while they brushed their teeth, their nightly routine ever since they moved in together.

"Think we'll ever be able to afford to buy a house?" Sage mused as she loaded up her toothbrush with paste. "We could build a huge bathroom with a double vanity."

Rosalie relaxed. Sage had apparently moved on from the subject of Casey.

"But then I wouldn't be able to do this," Rosalie pointed out as she bumped Sage's hip with her own. "Or this."

She reached over and squeezed her ass.

"That *is* a compelling argument," Sage admitted. "But remember that time we both tried to rinse at the same time and you spat your toothpaste on the back of my head?"

Rosalie shook her head. "You're never going to let me live that down."

"Hell no, I'm not."

They both rinsed – more carefully ever since that incident. Then Rosalie said, "Don't forget your meds, babe," and kissed Sage's cheek before leaving the bathroom.

They still hadn't talked about Sage's symptoms, if she was having more of them. Rosalie strongly suspected she was, but Sage was an adult and there was only so much she could do, only so far she could push her before Sage started pushing back. Rosalie had learned that lesson courtesy of her father, who always did whatever he damn well pleased no matter how much she begged him to take care of himself.

Taking the decision away only made things worse, but a gentle reminder here and there? It seemed to help.

"Bear, where are you?" she called into the already dark living room.

She heard his nails clicking across the hardwood toward her and he appeared in the doorway.

"Ready for bed?" she asked. She must have said it in too enthusiastic a tone, because his tail started wagging as if he'd just gotten an invitation to the dog park. "No, not play, bed."

"Oh, you've done it now," Sage called from the bathroom. "You said the P-word."

Bear snatched the nearest toy, a thick rope that he just loved to soak in slobber, and started whipping it around.

"No," Rosalie scolded. "Drop it."

Bear did not know all of his commands, or at least he pretended not to when it suited him. He kept whipping the rope around, and when she reached for it, he decided she was joining the game. He took off into the living room, and then the apartment filled with the sound of shattering glass.

"Oh shit." Rosalie reached for the light switch, and Sage was instantly at her side.

"What happened?"

"I think he knocked one of the centerpieces off the dining table."

Stella had dropped off three different options, cooked up by herself and Casey, the previous day. Casey's was a tasteful arrangement of Rosalie and Sage's favorite flowers in a vase that Sage had made herself. The other two... well, it was obvious which ones Stella had made.

"Shit, one of them has Jordan almonds in it – those contain chocolate," Sage said.

"Bear, come," Rosalie ordered.

"I'll get the broom." Sage headed for the closet in the kitchen.

Rosalie grabbed Bear by the collar, leading him away from the puddle of broken glass and yes, Jordan almonds, feathers and gawdy plastic diamonds. And behind him, there was a trail of bloody footprints.

"Oh no, my poor baby!"

"What?" Sage asked, appearing with the broom, eyes wide. She spotted the blood. "Did he cut his paw pad?"

"He's bleeding a lot," Rosalie said, scooping him up.

CARA MALONE

"And he might have eaten some of the almonds, I don't know."

Sage inspected his foot, then used the bottom of her T-shirt to try to apply pressure and stop the blood flow.

"How bad is it?" Rosalie asked.

"My shirt's already soaked. I think he needs stitches, or whatever they do for paw pads," Sage said.

"Fuck, the vet's office is definitely closed by now." It was eleven p.m. and this was all new territory for Rosalie. She'd never had a pet more complicated than a goldfish as a kid because she'd had enough on her plate already. "What do we do?"

"We have to take him to the emergency veterinary hospital," Sage said. "Do you think he ate chocolate? Shit, we should have put that one on top of the fridge or something."

"We were distracted, trying not to let Stella get wind of the bridal shower," Rosalie said, although that excuse didn't actually detract from the guilt. "I didn't see him eating anything, but he's fast."

"Let's go," Sage said, taking Bear out of Rosalie's arms so she could keep pressure on his paw while Rosalie drove.

The emergency vet was a twenty-minute drive away, and the worst twenty minutes of Rosalie's life – even with everything Stella had put them through in the last few months. Bear was squirming in Sage's arms in the back seat, crying and trying to free his paw, and Sage was keeping Rosalie updated on the mess they were making back there.

186

"I think the bleeding has slowed, but we're really fucking up your upholstery."

"I don't care about the seats. How much blood can a dog lose before it's dangerous, do you think?"

"I don't think we're there yet," Sage said, trying to be reassuring. "It looks like a horror movie back here, but it's his paw – it's not like he hit a major artery."

When they got to the veterinary hospital, though, the staff treated Bear as if he had. Rosalie had phoned ahead to let them know they were coming, and the staff greeted the three of them in the lobby, ready for action. In a blur of vet techs and questions and paperwork, they took Bear into an examination room and pointed Rosalie and Sage to a small waiting area, and then suddenly they were alone.

The room was empty at this time of night, and there wasn't even any ambient music playing. It was dead silent as Rosalie sank down into one of the chairs, a clipboard full of new patient paperwork in her lap.

Sage sat beside her. "You okay?"

Rosalie nodded. "Terrified, but he'll be okay, right?"

"It's just a cut," Sage said. "They'll stitch him up and he'll be fine."

"And we told them there's a possibility he could have eaten some chocolate, right?" Rosalie honestly couldn't remember, and she wondered if this was what it felt like when Sage had brain fog. That conversation *just* happened, but she could only recall it in bits and pieces, scattered and out of order.

"Yes, we told them."

"Honestly, who the fuck puts Jordan almonds in a centerpiece?"

"Someone who's lost touch with reality," Sage smiled.

Rosalie put her head on Sage's shoulder, then caught a whiff of metallic blood and lifted her head. "Oh my god, you look awful."

"Gee, thanks," Sage laughed. She had a softball-sized blood spot on the front of her shirt, and that was definitely not coming out in the laundry.

"We better fill this out," Rosalie said, remembering the clipboard in her hands. It asked all the usual information – Bear's age and breed, allergies and medical history – and the vet techs had said they'd come for it in a few minutes. Filling it out was a pretty good distraction, and Rosalie felt a little bit calmer by the time she was done.

That calmness evaporated when the door opened and the vet tech stepped into the waiting room.

"How is he?" she asked, popping out of her seat.

"Since there's the possibility he swallowed glass shards, we can't induce vomiting like we normally do for chocolate ingestion. The vet is X-raying his stomach now," the vet tech said. "And his paw will need stitches."

He took the form, glancing over it quickly, then told them to expect at least another hour's wait. He went back into the exam room and Sage looked at Rosalie.

"That's encouraging, right?"

"I guess so."

"Come on, sit down with me." They took their seats again and Sage wrapped her arm around Rosalie's shoulder, resting her head on top of Rosalie's. "I hate hospi-tals... even veterinary ones. That antiseptic smell..."

"I don't think it's anyone's favorite," Rosalie added, although Sage had very specific reasons for disliking hospitals. Hopefully this wasn't bringing back too many traumatic memories for her.

"I saw you and my mom standing together for a while at the bridal shower," Sage said. "What did you talk about?"

She was looking for a distraction – Rosalie could tell. "You, mostly. How proud we are of you growing your business, how sharp you're gonna look in your wedding suit... how sweet you are with Willow's kids and how you're gonna make a great parent someday."

Sage snorted. "Someday far into the future. I can't even handle a dog emergency without looking like I survived a slasher flick."

"I think you handled it just right."

They fell silent and Rosalie kept thinking about the bridal shower. Sage had disappeared for a while and Rosalie could tell that the whole thing was a lot for her to handle, but they got through it with grace. She just hoped the same would be true of the wedding, which would be the bridal shower times ten in terms of people, noise, small talk, stress.

They *could* handle it. They could handle anything as long as they were together.

With nothing to do other than worry about Bear, Rosalie started stewing over her conversation with Casey again. Casey had tried to talk to her at the shower, asked to go out and grab a coffee or something and talk, but Rosalie had given her the cold shoulder.

Honestly, her own best friend had the gall to tell her not to marry the woman of her dreams, to get out while she still could.

And Rosalie couldn't even vent about it, because Sage was the one she always turned to for that. Sage could never know what Casey said, or they'd end up hating each other forever.

Her best friend and her wife.

Rosalie couldn't have that.

She forced it from her mind, and thankfully a happier memory resurfaced. "Oh, babe, did I tell you what Robbie said at the shower? He wanted to know if, when the time came, it would be okay for him to take a bridal bath because he doesn't like showers."

She chuckled, and Sage didn't respond. Rosalie noticed that her chest was rising and falling evenly, and she could feel her warm, minty toothpaste breath against her skin.

Her meds really knocked her on her ass – that was why she took them right before bed, because she had about twenty minutes before she just couldn't keep her eyes open a moment longer. Adrenaline had carried her a bit further tonight, but she must have hit her limit.

Rosalie adjusted herself around Sage, carefully extracting herself, sitting up and laying Sage's head on her shoulder. "Love you, babe."

30

SAGE

"Babe, time to wake up."

Sage's eyes fluttered open to the sensation of Rosalie shaking her gently, her voice growing more insistent. "Hmm?"

"The vet is here."

"Vet?"

Groggily, she looked around and saw not her bedroom but a waiting room painted in 1980s pastels with big art prints of dogs and cats. Much more slowly than she would have liked, her brain caught up to the situation and she remembered that they were at the veterinary hospital.

That Bear cut his paw. And maybe ate chocolate, or even swallowed glass.

And then she saw that a woman in a white coat was standing in front of her, patiently waiting for Sage to get ahold of her mental faculties. How embarrassing.

"How is he?" she asked as she and Rosalie stood.

"He's just fine," the vet reassured them. "We put five stitches in his paw so you'll need to monitor the site, try to keep his weight off it."

Sage resisted the urge to roll her eyes. How would that be possible?

"And you'll need to make an appointment with your regular vet to have the stitches removed in two weeks," the vet went on.

"What about the glass?" Rosalie asked. "And the chocolate?"

"We didn't see any glass on the X-ray, which is good, and we gave him activated charcoal just in case he ingested any chocolate. However–" *Here it comes.* "–he did swallow what looks like a large plastic diamond."

Now Rosalie was the one to roll her eyes as she explained about the centerpiece.

"Well, it could be an issue if he doesn't pass it, but I think he will. You'll just need to keep an eye on his output and make sure that he does."

Output... code for *sift through his shit for the next few days.* Lovely.

"So he can go home?" Rosalie asked.

"Yes, I'll have my tech bring him out. Meanwhile, you can go to the desk and settle the bill."

Well, that was something Sage wanted to do even less than "monitoring Bear's output." Rosalie thanked the vet, who disappeared back into the exam room, and then they turned to each other.

"Good news, all in all," Rosalie concluded.

"Yeah, I think we got lucky... I'll take on some more

clients to cover this. I can't even guess how much emergency stitches and an X-ray in the middle of the night are going to cost."

"Don't worry about it," Rosalie said. "We'll figure it out together."

She took Sage's hand and they went out to the lobby, where a receptionist was waiting to empty their wallets.

"How long was I out for?" Sage asked as they walked.

"About an hour."

"I'm really sorry. I didn't mean to fall asleep."

"It's okay, I know your meds knock you out." Rosalie squeezed her hand reassuringly.

But Sage wasn't willing to let herself off the hook that easily. "It's not that I wasn't worried about Bear. And I shouldn't have made you sit there with no one to talk to that whole time."

"It's fine," Rosalie tried to insist. Then she turned to the receptionist. "Hi."

It wasn't fine, though. Sage felt like a shitty partner *and* a shitty dog parent. She should have been there for Rosalie, whether Rosalie wanted to let her off the hook or not, and it was frustrating as hell that her meds were interfering with that ability.

"...nine hundred..." She tuned back into the conversation just in time to hear their grand total – or at least she hoped that was the grand total.

"Here we are!"

Sage's head swam as a voice called over her shoulder, then she realized that the vet tech was carrying Bear into the lobby. Rosalie immediately abandoned the reception desk and went over to scoop him up.

"My poor baby," she cooed, inspecting his bandaged paw as he sleepily licked her cheek.

"He should still be feeling the sedative for another couple hours," the vet tech explained. "He'll sleep well tonight for sure."

Bear's eyes were only half open and Sage wondered if that was how she looked when she conked out from her meds. Rosalie brought him over and Sage let him lick her hand, then the receptionist asked if they wanted to set up a payment plan.

Which would go on top of the payment plans they'd set up for their wedding venue, and the photographer, and the DJ who was still expensive despite being far cheaper than a band...

"I'll pay it," Sage decided, taking out her wallet.

"Babe," Rosalie objected.

"I've got it," she insisted, handing the receptionist her debit card.

When the woman turned away to run the card, Rosalie lowered her voice and asked, "Do you have nine hundred dollars?"

"Don't worry about it," Sage said, kissing her forehead.

She *did* have nine hundred dollars. What she didn't have anymore was enough money to cover their airfare to Amsterdam, so that was a problem. At least there wasn't one more payment plan hanging around their necks.

The receptionist handed her card back, and Sage

turned to Rosalie, standing a little taller. "Okay, should we go home now?"

"Thank you," Rosalie said. "For doing that. And yes, let's go home. You and Bear can crash in the back seat while I drive."

Sage took Bear from her arms when they reached the car and climbed into the back seat with him. She laid him carefully beside her, then clicked her seatbelt in place.

And promptly fell asleep with her head against the window before she even heard the engine turn on.

31

ROSALIE

R osalie let out a sigh as she stared at the, erm,
chocolate soft serve that Bear was dishing up on
the lawn in front of the apartment.

The only good thing about his emergency trip to the
veterinary hospital was that it happened on a Friday
night, which meant she could dedicate her entire
weekend to keeping an eye on him and making sure he
recovered.

And closely scrutinizing his poop.

Ah, the joys of having a pet.

It was Saturday afternoon and apart from a brief nap
on the couch after lunch, she hadn't slept. She felt worn
down and like somebody had turned up the gravity, and
not just because she was worrying about Bear.

It was everything, compressing around her. And she
couldn't vent to Sage about it because the last thing she
wanted was to A, put even more stress on her incredible

but somewhat delicate fiancée, or B, make her feel like any of this was her fault.

Besides, Sage wasn't here even if she had wanted to talk. She'd gotten a call from a client whose car was stuck in his garage, not starting, and dashed off to make a few bucks to cover the vet expenses.

Or that was what she said, at least.

"She *did* just shell out nine hundred dollars for you and she wants to build back her savings. I shouldn't be suspicious," Rosalie told Bear. "She doesn't deserve that..." She let out another sigh and added, "But sometimes it's hard not to be."

How many times had her dad told her that he was just going over to Benny's house to help him install a ceiling fan or some other equally unlikely scenario, only to come home reeking of stale beer? Not that alcoholism and schizophrenia were anything alike, but any whiff of secrecy had a tendency to set Rosalie's teeth on edge.

Bear stood up and started kicking at the grass, proud of his work, and Rosalie tugged his leash to move him away from it.

"Any luck?" she asked.

The unpleasant business of inspecting it ensued, and she could at least find a silver lining in the fact that the plastic diamond he'd eaten was large – no need for rubber gloves and sifting.

"Not yet," she said. "Come on, let's go change your dressing."

His paw was doing well so far, still tender whenever she

197

tried to touch it, but the stitches looked good. She and Bear were sitting on the floor in the bathroom finishing up when Rosalie heard the apartment door open, and then Sage was in the bathroom doorway, holding a drug store shopping bag.

"How's the patient?"

"Good, still no diamond but his paw looks so much better today." Rosalie gave Bear the command to shake so Sage could see it, which he ignored, and then she let him trot off into the apartment. "Did you get your meds refilled?"

Sage looked at the bag. "Oh, no... I have plenty. I bought carpet cleaner to get the blood stain out of the living room floor, and while I was there..." She set the bag on the counter and pulled out a couple jars of hair dye – bright blue and bright pink.

Rosalie smirked. "Planning your Harley Quinn Halloween costume already? I don't think your hair is quite long enough to pull off the pigtails."

"Actually, I was thinking we could do something fun, lift our spirits. We've had a rough couple of months," Sage said. "I remember you said you always wondered what you'd look like with pink hair so I got that for you and blue for me, but we can switch if you want."

Rosalie laughed. "You want us to dye our hair less than a month before the wedding? Stella will shit a diamond of her own."

"Hey, it's *our* wedding. If we want to have colored hair, that's our call," Sage said. Then a smile broke across her face as she pointed to the pink jar. "Besides, it's temporary. It'll wash out in a day or two."

Rosalie relaxed. "Well, you could have led with that. Okay, let's do it. Sit."

She pointed to the edge of the tub, and Sage asked with a laugh, "Why am I the guinea pig who has to go first?"

"Because it was your idea," Rosalie said with a smirk. She picked up the blue dye, reading the instructions.

She had plastic gloves on and neon-blue goop all over her hands when Bear came back and plopped down in the doorway to watch, and Sage said, "If there's leftover dye, we should totally give Bear a makeover."

"We could mix them – blue for you, pink for me, purple dog."

"Too bad we're not getting married during Pride, we'd make a great bi flag."

"We'll remember it for next time," Rosalie promised, smoothing the goop over Sage's blonde hair.

"How's it look?"

"Like a Smurf took a dump on your head," Rosalie laughed. Sage was right, they needed to make time for fun, and this was the perfect thing.

"Gross."

"Sorry, I have poo on my mind for *some* reason," Rosalie said, side-eyeing Bear.

"I'll handle the next potty break," Sage promised.

"Oh, did you get your client's car working?" Rosalie asked, then bit her lip. Did she really want to know, or was she just prying, looking for any inconsistencies in Sage's story?

"Yeah, it was just a dead battery," Sage explained.

"But he was nosed into the garage so we had to put it in neutral and push it out to the driveway before I could jump it."

Rosalie focused on applying the dye, trying not to get too much of it on Sage's skin.

After a few moments of concentration, Sage said, "I was thinking maybe I should try a different medication for a while... or stop. Just till after the wedding."

"Babe..."

"I hate that I fell asleep in the middle of Bear's emergency – twice."

"But–"

"It's not like my symptoms would come back overnight or anything," Sage said. "And sometimes they don't come back at all. I've been doing some research and sometimes hallucinations, delusions, symptoms like that improve over time. And I'm a lot better at identifying and ignoring them now anyway. Maybe those meds were something I needed when I was younger, but now I'm sedating myself every night for no reason. Plus, you know I how hard it is for me to get my work done when I'm having muscle spasms..."

Rosalie just let Sage talk, all the while chewing on her lower lip like it needed to be taught a lesson. She knew from talking to Sage, and from all the people she'd interviewed for her column, that it was pretty common for people with mental health conditions to think this way – the meds were working so well they started to question whether they even needed them. She also knew that simply saying no would not be productive. It wasn't her call to make.

So she let Sage voice her concerns, and then she said, "When's your next psychiatrist appointment? You should talk to Dr. Khan if you want to change your meds."

"Not until after the wedding," Sage frowned. "But I want to be clear-headed *for* the wedding."

"Well, maybe you can move up your appointment–"

Sage's phone started ringing and she shifted on the edge of the tub, pulling it out of her pocket. "Oh god, it's Stella."

"Ignore it," Rosalie suggested. "We're having us time."

Sage set her phone down on the counter, and it kept ringing. "Yeah, but what if she needs us to make a decision?"

"We'll make it tomorrow, or call her back later today."

"She'll probably make the decision without us, and you know it won't be what we want."

Rosalie sighed. Sage was right. "Okay, answer it."

Sage picked up the phone again and accepted the video call. Stella's face appeared on the screen, her brows already knit with worry, but when she saw Sage's hair, her jaw dropped.

"What did you do?!"

"Stella, it's–"

"Your hair is *blue* and you do this a month before the wedding?" Stella was absolutely apoplectic. "It's not even the right shade to match your theme! How could you do this? *Are you crazy?!*"

Rosalie snatched the phone out of Sage's hand, accidentally smearing it with goop. She didn't care – they'd find the money for a new phone if they had to. This was the last straw. "Never talk to my fiancée like that again, Stella."

"But she–"

"Yes, I know, I'm the one who's dying it," she said, seething. "And in case you haven't noticed, *we're* the ones getting married, not you. If we want to unicycle down the aisle in matching clown costumes, that's our choice."

"Ros–"

"Stella, you're fired," she said, and suddenly the gravity dial got turned back down, right where it should be.

"Oh my god, you're so fired," Sage agreed, sounding just as relieved as Rosalie.

Stella started whining, or maybe she was shrieking. Either way, she wasn't making words, just letting stunned sounds come out of her mouth. Rosalie's finger moved over the *End Call* button, but before she could hit it, Stella managed to spit, "There isn't going to be a wedding anyway."

"What's that supposed to mean?" Rosalie asked.

"I called to tell you the venue just cancelled our contract," Stella said. "You and your crazy family made such a scene at the tasting, they don't want you anymore. So good luck with that a month before the wedding, without a planner."

She ended the call, robbing Rosalie of the satisfaction.

Rosalie handed her the phone, and Sage grabbed a handful of tissues to try to clean it up.

"Sorry," she said.

"It'll come off," Sage answered, showing her a tissue full of goop.

"Not that... all of this." Rosalie sank down on the closed toilet lid. "Have we been doomed from the start?"

SAGE

Doomed.

That word throbbed in Sage's head like an aneurysm threatening to burst. With every passing day, it felt more appropriate.

Every single step of the wedding planning process had been an unmitigated disaster. With less than a month to go, the whole event was crumbling around them. Rosalie was obviously in some kind of fight with Casey, but she wouldn't tell Sage what it was about, and there was another thing that wouldn't stop nagging at her.

Rosalie didn't want to call Angela Mom, and she also didn't seem to want Sage to have anything to do with her dad. She'd seated him at the complete opposite end of the table at that menu tasting, and she hadn't even invited Sage the day she told him they were engaged.

It was like Rosalie was ashamed of her.

That was a fear that had whispered in the back of her mind since the start. She'd only recently started allowing it to speak out loud. Because that was exactly what it felt like. Rosalie didn't want Sage to spend too much time with her dad because she and Sage both knew Sage wasn't good enough for her.

She couldn't plan a wedding without the world's worst wedding planner babysitting her. She couldn't juggle a full-time job and her symptoms at the same time. She couldn't even be trusted to have a little fun without fucking it up, because three days and five shampoos later, her hair was *still* blue.

"It's pretty," Rosalie tried to reassure her when she caught Sage frowning into the mirror. She ran her fingers through Sage's short hair, teasing the nape of her neck. The color had faded from its original neon blue to something approaching pastel, but it was still very visibly colored. "It's probably just because you have such light blonde hair. The dye... stuck, or something."

They hadn't gotten around to Rosalie's pink dye that first night after Stella's call, and when Sage's color wouldn't wash out, they'd decided against it.

"The one thing we *do* have is a photographer and my hair is going to be fucking blue in all our wedding photos," Sage groaned.

"So what's wrong with that?" Rosalie asked. It was a nice try, an attempt to reassure her, but Sage knew it wasn't what Rosalie really wanted. Who would?

"Maybe I can bleach it."

"We still have two and a half weeks," Rosalie reminded her, leaning in to attempt a kiss that Sage was too full of self-pity to reciprocate. "Just give it time."

And so she did.

She walked Bear and waited for him to produce a diamond, which he finally did the next morning.

She and Rosalie worked on trying – unsuccessfully – to book a new venue. They started making contingency plans to use Sage's parents' back yard, and they'd order an obscene amount of Giovanni's Pizza for the reception if they had to.

Sage went to the garage and changed oil and rotated tires like her life depended on it, keeping a close eye on her bank account and the fact that her savings was not growing at nearly the rate it needed to. She'd done the math, she thought she could make it happen, and so she'd gone ahead and booked their honeymoon to the Netherlands the night they went to Casey's place for pizza. And now she was on the hook for five grand that she didn't exactly have on hand.

Five grand that she had to come up with before their flight, or else they weren't going anywhere and Sage would be out all the money she'd already put down as a deposit.

And to top it all off, now that word kept echoing in her head, and sometimes over her shoulder. *Doomed, doomed, doomed.*

Did Rosalie even still want to marry her? Had she finally figured out Sage wasn't good enough for her?

Sage was too afraid to ask.

She got her appointment with Dr. Khan moved up like Rosalie suggested. A week and a half before the wedding, she went to her doctor's office, still determined to change her meds. There was just enough time to get off them so she could be as clear-headed and alert as possible on the big day.

"Are you excited?" Dr. Khan asked while they made small talk at the beginning of the appointment.

Sage hesitated, then felt guilty about it, and of course Dr. Khan noticed.

"Nervous?" she guessed.

"Rosalie is the most amazing woman I've ever met and I want nothing more than to be her wife," Sage said.

"But?"

Sage let out a huff. "This whole process has been a nightmare. I'm a little worried she doesn't feel the same way after everything we've been through. A lot of it is my fault, and that's why I wanted to talk to you about stopping my meds."

Dr. Khan blinked. "Okay, let's take a couple of steps back. How will stopping your medication ensure your fiancée wants to marry you?"

"Well, who the hell wants to marry a crazy person who has to take antipsychotics every night?"

"Sage, you're not–"

"Yeah, I know," she waved her off. They'd had that conversation many times over the years, shifting her mindset and learning not to feel othered or less-than because of her diagnosis. And most of the time it worked – lately, though? Her schizophrenia felt like a chasm between herself and Rosalie. "Look, I've been doing a lot of reading lately. There's a large portion of people with schizophrenia who recover over time and don't even need antipsychotics anymore – some of them are off those meds within a year of diagnosis, but I've been taking mine for almost a decade!"

She'd been seeing Dr. Khan that long, too.

"Maybe I should get a second opinion," she added, biting her tongue to keep herself from insinuating what was in the back of her mind – that her doctor was keeping her on meds she didn't need because of what, laziness? The kickbacks from the pharmaceutical industry?

"You're always free to do that," Dr. Khan said. "May I point something out, though?"

Sage nodded.

"You just said that your experiences with wedding planning have been a nightmare. I'm guessing that comes with quite a bit of stress?" she asked, and Sage nodded again. "And we know that stress is a major trigger for breakthrough symptoms. Have you been experiencing any hallucinations, delusions?"

"No," Sage said.

"Anything you've needed to do a reality check with Rosalie on?" the doctor pressed. "Chatter over your shoulder, bad smells? Trouble finishing your thoughts? Those were the things you struggled with the most before we decided on your current medication."

She *had* started to notice an unpleasant smell in the apartment lately, and Rosalie could never smell it. But they had a dog – Bear probably just rolled in something gross and tracked it into the house.

"No," Sage insisted. "I just don't think I need my meds anymore. I hate how they make me feel. I'm always tired, and it's really hard to hold a wrench steady when your muscles are twitching all over the place."

"We've tried tapering off in the past," Dr. Khan reminded her, which wasn't a very pleasant memory – the tapering itself, or the symptoms which came back to the surface.

But that had been *years* ago. "Don't you think it's worth trying again?" Sage asked.

"Well, we can always try a different medication if the side effects of this one are unmanageable," Dr. Khan suggested. "And I'm not telling you it's out of the question to stop your medication – we can try again if you want to. I'm just suggesting that now might not be the best time for it, with the wedding coming up so soon."

"I want to be *present* for my wedding, and the honeymoon," Sage argued. "I don't want to be tied to my medicine cabinet. I just want to live my life."

"I hear you," Dr. Khan said. God, she was annoyingly understanding. "And I'd like to help you live your best life, whether that means taking this medication or another one, or none at all. But we have to go slow and be patient while we figure that out, okay?"

Sage grumbled and didn't give a direct answer.

"And I know you've been busy, but I'd love to see you come back to group sessions."

"I will," Sage promised. "After the wedding."

Dr. Khan asked, "Have you been taking your medication as directed?"

"Yes," she said, then rolled her eyes. "I mean, I've

skipped a few doses here and there – wedding chaos, you know?"

"How many is a few?" Dr. Khan asked.

Should she lie? Sage had known the doctor for almost a decade now and they had a good working relationship... but the power Dr. Khan had to put Sage on an involuntary hold if she felt it was necessary... or if she was feeling vindictive, maybe about Sage threatening to get a new doctor? It was never completely out of her mind when she came to these appointments.

"Maybe one or two," Sage fibbed. Taking her meds was such a routine thing that she barely ever thought about it anymore, and that meant she sometimes didn't notice when something distracted her into missing a dose. It had definitely been more than twice, though. "Not many."

"And when was your last missed dose?"

"A few weeks ago," Sage said. Was that true? No, she'd intentionally skipped her dose the day after Bear's accident because she wanted to make sure she was fully alert just in case something happened again. She'd been spotty all week. "I promise I'll do better."

"I'd appreciate that," Dr. Khan said. "And we can talk about changing your medication after you get back from the honeymoon. Why don't you tell me about that, switch to a happy topic for a bit?"

She was trying to stall for time. She'd probably pushed some kind of panic button within reach of her chair and was just waiting for the paramedics to arrive and cart Sage off to the psych ward, and she thought asking Sage about the honeymoon would keep her distracted enough to keep sitting here patiently.

"Oh, look at the time," she said, glancing at her smart watch. "My appointment's almost over, I'll get out of your hair."

"Sage–"

She was already halfway to the door. "We'll talk after the wedding, thanks, doc."

Sage only felt a *little* silly when her feet hit the pavement outside the office building, breathing heavy from her rapid exit. Okay, so Dr. Khan had never sent goons to drag Sage away before and she *probably* wasn't planning on it today either.

Better safe than sorry, though.

Besides, Sage had a client coming to the garage in half an hour, and more than a thousand dollars left to earn if she was going to make the honeymoon happen.

33

ROSALIE

"How did we get here?" It was the thought that had been playing on repeat in Rosalie's mind for the last eight hours, and finally she said it out loud.

Sage didn't even acknowledge the question. She was busy pacing back and forth across the very small floor space of the private room they were in at the back of the hospital emergency department, like a caged animal. No doubt, that was exactly what she felt like, and the more she paced, the more anxious Rosalie felt too.

They'd been here all night already, waiting for a doctor, waiting for an evaluation, waiting for the dose of antipsychotic medication Sage had agreed to take to kick in. It was two days before what was supposed to be their wedding day, and Rosalie couldn't imagine it still happening like it was supposed to.

Not that *any* of it had gone according to plan, at any point in the process. It had been moved to Sage's parents' back yard, they'd sent out dozens of texts and Facebook messages letting people know about the change of venue, and Rosalie wasn't even speaking to her maid of honor.

This was just the cherry on top.

"I want to leave," Sage said. "I don't like it here. You're going to leave me here to rot."

"I'm not going anywhere, babe," Rosalie tried to reassure her, but she could see in Sage's eyes that she wasn't in a state to be convinced.

Honestly, how the *fuck* did they get here?

It felt like just yesterday they were at the pier, having banh mi and watching Bear splash through the surf, and everything was right with the world. Now Sage was having the worst symptoms she'd experienced since they began dating, not quite in full psychosis but well on her way if she didn't get proper intervention, and it felt like Rosalie's fault.

She shouldn't have agreed to a big, stressful wedding.

She should have paid closer attention, noticed the signs sooner.

She should have taken better care of her.

Rosalie could practically hear each one of those accusations in her aunt Kathy's voice, it was all so similar to the way things were with her dad growing up. A heavy, uncomfortable pit was forming in her stomach. Aunt Kathy was right all along.

"Babe, do you want to sit for a few minutes?" she asked gently. "It's four in the morning, you must be tired."

"I want to go home," Sage said.

"I know." Rosalie frowned and hugged her arms to her belly.

She was sitting on a bench bolted to the wall and it was the only furniture in the room – more like a jail cell than a hospital room, and doing absolutely nothing for the anxiety that kept Sage pacing back and forth across the floor.

Not all ERs were equipped with rooms like this, for patients who may be a danger to themselves or others. In some ways, they were lucky they had one nearby. Rosalie knew about it because she'd written an article on the subject a few months ago and she'd toured this very room at the time. But it felt very different from the other side of the plexiglass.

At least she was allowed to stay with Sage in the room. Sage's parents were at the hospital too, in a waiting room down the hall. Rosalie had called them right after she convinced Sage to come here, but the nurses had drawn a firm line at a single visitor in the room with her. Angela and Scott popped by every hour or so to check on the two of them, and Rosalie had tried several times to get them to go home, promising she'd call if there were any developments. Angela wouldn't hear of it, though.

"Are you hungry?" Rosalie asked Sage. Her own stomach was gnawing at itself – they'd been here for what felt like an eternity.

She wasn't surprised when Sage shook her head. "I can't eat right now."

"Me neither," Rosalie agreed. This place was the worst kind of purgatory, and that was from the perspective of someone who got to go home whenever she wanted. Was Sage coming home at the end of the day? That was still very much up in the air.

"This is exactly why I didn't want to ask Dr. Khan about my meds," Sage said, abruptly spinning to face Rosalie. "She doesn't want me to stop taking them and bam, now I'm here getting them forced down my throat."

"You agreed with the ER doctor that it was a good idea for you to take them," Rosalie reminded her.

Sage had been acting increasingly erratic over the past few weeks, talking fast and moving around the apartment like a Tasmanian devil, trying to fix all the problems of the wedding by herself. She'd told Rosalie that Dr. Khan didn't want to adjust Sage's meds until after the wedding, and she'd also confessed to accidentally skipping a few doses lately.

Rosalie suspected that she'd skipped more than a few, and it was heartbreaking and terrifying and frustrating all at once, watching the love of her life make bad decisions she couldn't do anything about.

"I did agree, but they have me locked in a room – what am I going to say?" Sage started pacing again. "If I refused, they would have strapped me down and I am *not* doing that again."

"I don't want that to happen either," Rosalie said, though she had a sneaking suspicion Sage didn't believe her. It was like a switch had flipped in Sage's head. The minute Rosalie suggested they come here, she'd stopped being an ally and became an antagonist in Sage's mind. She could see Sage looking at her out of the corner of her eyes as she paced, like she didn't trust her enough to take her eyes off her.

No matter how many times Rosalie told herself – and the nurses told her – it was just the paranoia speaking, knowing that Sage didn't trust her felt like someone was cracking her chest open.

"Just give it time, let the medication take effect," one of the nicer ER nurses had told her. "If she's been off her meds for a while, the effect on her delusions won't be immediate, but she'll be calmer and more clear-headed in a couple of hours."

"Have you treated psychosis a lot?" Rosalie asked. They'd been standing in the hall while the doctor was in the room administering the medication.

"Yes, for a whole host of conditions," the nurse said. "Nobody likes being in that room, I won't try to tell you it's fun, but you will get through it – both of you."

"It feels like she hates me," Rosalie exhaled the fear that had been building its home in her belly.

"She doesn't," the nurse said. "She's not herself right now. I know it's easier said than done, but try not to take any of this personally. Just focus on getting through it."

It *was* easier said than done. All Rosalie wanted to do was wrap Sage up in her arms and protect her from the whole world *and* her own mind. But she couldn't. She couldn't even hug her fiancée because Sage seemed incapable of standing still right now.

All either of them could do was wait.

Finally, after the nice nurse's shift ended and a whole new staff arrived, a hospital psychiatrist showed up to evaluate Sage – and as luck would have it, her parents chose that exact moment to come check in, too.

The three of them came into the room together, and the doctor extended his hand to Sage and then Rosalie. "I'm Dr. Martin, I just met your parents in the hall."

Sage looked back and forth between the doctor and her parents. It was subtle, but Rosalie could see the suspicion in her eyes already, like they'd formed an alliance out there. Great start.

"Would you mind having a seat for me so I can do a quick exam?" Dr. Martin asked. Rosalie got off the bench so Sage could sit down and he examined her pupils. "How are you feeling?"

"Like a lab rat," Sage said.

"I read the overnight nurses' notes, but maybe you can tell me in your own words what brought you in," the doctor prompted as he continued his exam.

"Rosalie brought me in," Sage said. "She thinks I'm off my meds."

"Are you?"

"No, I just forgot a few doses here and there," Sage said.

Rosalie bit her lower lip, struggling against the urge to explain what she was seeing from her point of view. Sage's inability to sit still. The paranoia. How alarmingly fast it all came on. But the doctor hadn't asked her – she'd wait until he did.

Dr. Martin moved efficiently through each step of his evaluation, assessing Sage's physical and mental states. The whole thing took about half an hour, which felt sort of perfunctory after waiting all night for it. At the end, he took a step back from the bench to allow Sage to stand if she wanted. He asked, "Have you appointed a power of attorney, Sage?"

"That's me," Angela spoke up. "I have been for years."

Beside her, Rosalie tried not to register her surprise. Granted, it had never come up in conversation – which was an oversight, she saw now – and it made sense that Sage had appointed one of her parents back when she was first diagnosed... but it should be Rosalie now, right?

Or at least, it should be when they were married.

If we get married, that annoying, painful voice whispered.

The doctor nodded. "Well, I'm going to recommend that you're admitted – voluntarily, if you'll agree to it."

"Involuntarily if I don't agree?" Sage asked sardonically. "Doesn't feel like much of a choice, doc."

He ignored her comment, continuing. "There's a bed available upstairs, and your partner brought you in promptly so that's good news. It shouldn't be a long stay – just until you're compliant with your meds again."

"I am compliant, I just forgot," Sage argued. "I took them when they asked me to earlier, check my chart!"

Her eyes were wild now and there was that cracking open feeling in Rosalie's chest again. "Babe, I think you should listen to the doctor. You've been running yourself ragged lately – let them take care of you for a little while."

"We're getting married tomorrow," Sage said. "I can't miss my own wedding!"

"We'll reschedule," Angela reassured her.

"Can't have a wedding without one of the brides," her dad pointed out.

"Besides, it's not like we *have* much of a wedding to show up to," Rosalie said. She was going for levity, something to make Sage smile if only for a second. Sage was so good at that when Rosalie needed a break. Instead, it just sounded ominous.

"Please." Sage came over to Rosalie for the first time since they'd walked into that room. Her eyes were wide as saucers with tears welling in them, panic swimming just beneath the surface. "Don't make me do this. It's awful in there."

They were both crying now, and when Rosalie reached out to hug Sage, relief poured over her at the simple fact that Sage did not pull away.

"Take me home," Sage begged.

"I think you need to stay," Rosalie said softly. They were the worst six words she'd ever spoken to another person, but Sage did need this. "You've been struggling and I should have seen it sooner – I'm sorry for that. You just need a little bit of help getting back on track. That's all."

She felt Sage's arms clamp tight around her. "Don't leave me. I'll do better, I'll never skip another dose, I promise."

Rosalie was flat-out sobbing now, and her throat was so thick with tears it was hard to form the words to comfort her partner. "You'll be okay."

"What about Bear?" Sage asked as the doctor and her mom began prying her off Rosalie. "He's going to miss me."

"This is just for a few days," Rosalie said.

"He's going to wonder where I went," Sage continued as if she hadn't heard her.

As soon as Sage's arms broke away from around Rosalie's shoulders, she slumped down on the bench. She couldn't bring herself to watch them dragging her fiancée away, talking like this was the end for them.

Angela followed Sage and the doctor into the hall, and that left Rosalie with Scott. She didn't even notice he was still there until he put a hand on her shoulder.

"The first time is the worst," he said. "We had to do this a couple of times when she first got diagnosed, while we were figuring out which meds would work for her. I hoped we'd never have to be back here again."

Rosalie used the bottom of her T-shirt to wipe the tears and snot off her face, leaving her outsides looking like the hot mess she was on the inside. "I didn't want to bring her here."

"I know."

"I probably put off doing something longer than I should have, but... she's an adult, you know? I'm not her keeper, and I didn't want her to hate me."

"She does *not* hate you," Scott said. "I've never seen her so enamored with anyone as she is with you. And she *will* appreciate what you did for her tonight once she's able to process it."

"I couldn't get her to calm down," Rosalie said, flashing back to the second midnight emergency they'd had in as many weeks. Sage had been more keyed up than usual for days, but Rosalie wrote it off as wedding jitters. She'd written a lot of things off in the last few weeks and months. "She wouldn't come to bed. She was just pacing in the living room, talking about money for the honeymoon and it didn't make sense. She's been sleeping a lot less than usual and I should have taken that as a warning sign, but between the wedding and work and Bear and..."

"Do you know the number of times Angela and I said the words 'should have' when Sage was first diagnosed?" Scott laughed. "Hell, apply that to parenting in general – there's something for you two to look forward to."

He winked, but Rosalie was not in a laughing mood.

Scott squeezed her shoulder. "You did the right thing. And I'm really glad that Sage has you – because it's comforting knowing she has someone looking out for her, but more importantly because I know you're right for her."

"I'm trying."

"All any of us can do is try."

Scott sat down on the bench, the two of them waiting for Angela to return, and at last, Rosalie cracked a smile. "I think I understand Angela better now. I've always liked her, but I thought she was–"

She bit her tongue before she said something

insulting to her future father-in-law. Scott just laughed again and said, "Overbearing? Coddling? A helicopter parent?"

"Yes."

"Well, I'll get my wife to back off if you promise to look after yours," he said. "It's time we take a step back so that you two can step forward, anyway."

SAGE

Here again.

The antiseptic smell attempting to mask other, even less palatable odors. The unsettling cries and shouts of other patients in the throes of different kinds of crises. The harsh fluorescent lights that were impossible to escape from. The thin sheets and even thinner pillows on her bed.

Sage remembered it all keenly, even though years had passed since last time she was in a room like this, on the psychiatric ward of the hospital.

Last time was during a full-blown psychotic episode, before she and Dr. Khan got her meds adjusted correctly. She'd been terrified and confused and it felt like her heart raced with adrenaline the whole time she was there, until the medications finally started to do their job.

This time, she'd hardly moved a muscle in the thirty-six hours she'd been here, except to drag herself to the toilet a couple of times. She'd swung rapidly from manic paranoia to a crushing depression the minute Rosalie allowed the orderlies to drag her out of that ER cell. That was when it occurred to Sage that she was without a doubt going to miss her wedding, and maybe that was the only chance she'd get.

Rosalie wouldn't wait for her. Now that she'd seen what it was really like, what it really meant to live with Sage, she wouldn't stick around.

She probably started packing her bags the minute she got home. She might already be gone. There were no clocks in the rooms around here and although Sage had a vague sense that a day and a night had passed, it was easy to lose track. Especially when you didn't care that much in the first place.

"Sage?"

A soft voice broke through her melancholy, and she grunted in response. Her face was buried in the thin pillow and she didn't know if she'd just been lying there in a pool of her own self-pity or if she'd been drifting in and out of sleep. Was she awake now? What difference did it make?

"Sage, it's Dr. Khan," the voice came again. "I'd like to talk to you."

"Be my guest," Sage said into the pillow. She heard a chair scraping across the linoleum.

"I was sorry to hear that you were admitted," her doctor said. "I came as soon as my schedule allowed."

Sage didn't answer. It felt like it would be too much effort, require more energy than she had at her disposal.

"Can we talk about what happened?" Dr. Khan pressed. "Make a plan to get back on track?"

"There is no track," Sage groaned.

"What's that?" the doctor asked. "Sage, honey, I can't hear you with your face pressed into the pillow."

Sage let out a huff and shoved herself upright. The room was bright even though the overheads were mercifully turned off, and she thought she smelled breakfast meats somewhere down the hall. Morning, then. Dr. Khan sat in a molded plastic chair without any sharp corners so people like Sage couldn't use it to hurt themselves – or their doctors.

She *certainly* didn't have the energy for all of that.

"I said there is no track," she managed. "There's no train to put back on it if there was a track. It's all burning at the bottom of a ravine."

"And yet you're still here," Dr. Khan pointed out with a slight smile. "You must have jumped out at the last minute, and so there *is* still something worth saving."

God, that smirk was obnoxious. "I should have stayed on the train. There's no point if I don't have Rosalie."

"Who says you don't?"

"Come on, Dr. Khan, do you really think she's going to stick around after this? I'm missing our wedding as we speak!"

"Everything you've told me about Rosalie since you met her indicates that she cares a lot more about you than about a one-day event," Dr. Khan said. "She's educated herself extensively about your condition, and started educating others as well. You've both made a number of compromises all through the wedding planning process because you've kept each other's best interests in mind. And she brought you to get help when she saw you needed it."

"More like she dumped me here so she could run far away," Sage shot back. "Not that I blame her. Who could handle this?"

"Rosalie could," Dr. Khan responded instantly. "She loves you and she wants to be with you, and from what I saw in your patient records, she did the opposite of dumping you here and running."

Sage grunted, looking at her pillow and considering doing another face-first freefall into it.

Dr. Khan scooted a little closer. "Sage, you've been dealt a difficult hand with this condition, but not an impossible one, and I've seen you adapt and thrive over the past ten years. I'm really proud of how far you've come, especially when it comes to putting yourself out there. I know it was a struggle for you, and I don't want to see you push away someone you love, someone who loves you, because you're scared to take this next step. Yes, living with schizophrenia *and* a significant other is more challenging than living with it alone, but you have a good support system, good coping skills, and a partner who wants to do everything she can to be there for you. Let her."

The doctor fell silent, and Sage leaned back against her headboard.

Time became nebulous again as Sage's brain slowly waded through what Dr. Khan had said, trying to make sense of it in spite of the brain fog that was present more often than not lately. Maybe it was an hour, but probably it was only a few minutes because Dr. Khan was still there.

At last, she said, "Okay. Let's rebuild the track."

35

ROSALIE

Rosalie sank down into a café chair at an outdoor table, Bear curling up at her feet. She felt like she hadn't slept in days, although she knew that wasn't entirely true – she'd nodded off here and there, including once at her desk. Embarrassingly, it had been Hasan who woke her, although he was kind about it. He knew she was struggling, even though she hadn't shared details, and he'd told her to take the afternoon off.

Instead of going home to sulk in her empty apartment, she'd finally accepted Casey's repeated pleas to get coffee and talk.

She swung home to pick up Bear, and now Casey was inside the coffee shop placing their orders. Rosalie wasn't thrilled about the meeting, not feeling particularly forgiving at the moment, but she *was* excited about the caffeine she sorely needed.

When Casey returned, she had iced coffees for each of them, and a puppuccino for Bear. Rosalie couldn't help smiling as she watched him scarf down the whipped cream in a single greedy gulp.

"You know he's not the one you're supposed to be sucking up to, right?"

"Yeah, but I figured it couldn't hurt," Casey said, sitting down and distributing their coffees. "Thanks for meeting me."

"I wasn't excited about being alone right now, and Hasan wouldn't let me stay at work," Rosalie explained. Casey had taken a hasty lunch break from her own job as soon as Rosalie called her.

"You're pretty worried about Sage, huh?"

"I mean, I know she's in good hands, and Dr. Khan has been in to see her," Rosalie said. "She'll be okay... but seeing her like that, hearing her accuse me of dumping her there like I was trying to get rid of her... it was awful."

"How long do the doctors think she'll need to stay?" Casey asked.

Damn her... Rosalie had been looking forward to telling her off for what she said at pizza night, but she also really needed her best friend right now and Casey was making it so easy to just fall right back into old dynamics. "I'm still mad at you," she warned her.

"I understand."

"And I want to talk about that."

"Of course."

Rosalie let out a sigh. "Dr. Khan was hopeful it would only be a couple of days – get the most acute symptoms under control, and then just monitor her at home after that, extra appointments until she's back on track. She'll be more comfortable at home and it'll be easier on all of us that way."

"Did she go off her meds?" Casey asked.

"Not completely," Rosalie said. "But she skipped enough of them that it threw her off balance. Add to that all the stress of the wedding, and Bear needing to go to the emergency vet... it's been a lot for both of us."

"Wait, what happened to Bear?" Casey reached down to scratch behind his ears and he rolled onto his back for belly rubs – something he did for very few people.

"Right, we weren't talking," Rosalie remembered. She filled Casey in on all the dirty details – including the fact that the plastic diamond had come out right in front of a couple of neighborhood kids who'd happened to be passing by. "Their eyes went so wide, like we had a jewel-dispensing dog. I'd actually find it funny if it wasn't for the thousand-dollar vet bill."

Casey chuckled along with her. "If only it were a real diamond." She sat upright again and turned in her chair to fully face Rosalie. "Listen, I want to apologize to you – and to Sage, too. What I said was out of love and concern for you, but it also wasn't fair and it was pretty ignorant."

"Yeah, it was," Rosalie agreed.

"I've been reading up on schizophrenia, and watching a bunch of first-hand accounts on YouTube," she said. "I should have done that a year ago, but Sage always seemed so in control of it that it didn't feel real until recently."

"I know what you mean," Rosalie said. "I *did* do my

research, and it still didn't feel real. It didn't affect our lives all that much, until it did. But no matter how well she's managing her symptoms, she's always going to be living with chronic mental illness."

"And that scared me, for your sake," Casey said. "I don't know if I could handle that, so I was worried you might not want to either. But you're not me, plus I expressed my concern in all the wrong ways. Oh, and I was drunk and just got dumped."

"Maybe I shouldn't have held it against you for as long as I did..."

"But you've been under a lot of stress too," Casey said. "The truth is that no matter what hurdles the two of you have in your path, I know you can get over them. I've seen you together and I've seen you apart, and you're meant to be with each other. That much was obvious from the very first time you mentioned her."

Rosalie smiled at the memory. She and Casey had been having pizza a couple days after Sage rescued her on the highway, and she couldn't stop smiling. Casey had wrung every last detail of the encounter out of Rosalie, and she was just as excited for their Blue Whale Festival date as Rosalie.

"So you're behind us now?" Rosalie asked.

"One hundred percent," Casey said. "I'm sorry that I ever doubted you – either of you."

"Thank you." Rosalie drained her coffee and Casey offered to get her another, but she shook her head. "I probably should try to nap at some point this afternoon.

When Sage comes home, I need to be at the top of my game so I can be there for her."

"I'm here too," Casey reminded her. "All you need to do is call." She took a slower sip of her own coffee, then grimaced. "Although I do have some bad news."

"I can't take any more bad news," Rosalie said.

"I know... and maybe this is moot considering, you know, the wedding was supposed to be several days ago," Casey said. "How are you feeling about that, by the way?"

"Can't be helped," Rosalie said. "No sense in crying over it."

"Very chill," Casey eyed her suspiciously. "But okay."

"What's the bad news?" Rosalie braced herself.

"I should have told you before, but I didn't want to pile on, and we weren't even speaking... when I went to pick up my bridesmaid's dress a couple days before the wedding date, it was both the wrong color and the wrong size."

Rosalie tilted her head toward the sky and groaned. "Of course it was. Willow said hers was fine, I wonder what happened?"

"No clue," Casey said, getting out her phone and flipping to a photo she'd taken. She turned the screen to Rosalie. Casey was wearing the dress in the photo, which was pure white and hung halfway to her ankles with about a parachute's worth of fabric draped around her.

Rosalie started laughing. "You look like a weather balloon!"

"Gee, thanks."

"I'm sorry, but why is it white? Who the hell would want their bridal party to wear white?" Tears were streaking down her cheeks now. "Did they think you were one of the brides?"

"I don't know, but since we have time now, maybe I can take it to a tailor, have it cut down and dyed..."

"Hell, make it into two or three summer dresses for yourself," Rosalie said. "And just wear whatever you want to the wedding."

Casey smiled hopefully. "So, I'm still invited?"

"Yes, of course," Rosalie said. "You're my maid of honor." Then she rolled her eyes. "I mean, whatever version of a wedding we have at this point."

36

SAGE

This time leaving the hospital felt a lot different than the first, ten years before.

That first time, Sage was overcome with an incredible sense of loss – for the life she had before her diagnosis, for her pre-schizophrenia identity, for the concept of normalcy that seemed dead at that point.

This time, after nearly a week's stay, it was like she was standing on a precipice, *about* to lose everything.

It felt like not being able to catch her breath, no matter how many times she tried to take a full inhale.

"You take care of yourself now, okay?" the orderly who was pushing her wheelchair said as they emerged from the building.

"I'll try." Sage watched Rosalie's familiar black Civic pull up to the curb, her heart in her throat and her chest tight.

She stood, but before she could take more than a step toward the car, Rosalie burst out of the driver's side and

AGAINST ALL ODDS

ran around to meet her. Bear was on her heels, nearly tripping her several times in their mutual excitement to meet Sage.

"I missed you so much," Rosalie said, throwing her arms around Sage's neck. Bear was jumping at Sage's thigh, licking her hand until it was dripping, and Sage burst into tears.

"I missed you too," was all she could manage before her throat closed up.

"Ma'am? You can't park here," the parking attendant said.

"We're not," Rosalie assured him, but he wasn't happy with that.

"We need to keep traffic moving."

"Okay, okay," she said, taking Sage's hand.

They piled back in the car. Bear wound up in Sage's lap, attempting to lick every inch of her face, and Rosalie pulled away before the attendant got any angrier.

"Told you he wouldn't forget you," she said. "Where should we go? Are you hungry?"

"Starving," Sage said. The hospital food was edible, but it was nothing to get excited about. "But I really just want to go home."

"Let's get something to go, then," Rosalie said. "Burritos?"

"Sure."

It was one of their go-tos on nights when neither of them felt like cooking, and the idea of something familiar and delicious was comforting. It *almost* made Sage forget about the precipice.

Rosalie swung through the drive-through and they got back to the apartment about thirty minutes later. They didn't do a ton of talking in the car – Rosalie just held Sage's hand and Sage silently savored her presence. When they got home, they sat on the couch and Bear glued himself to Sage's lap while she wolfed down her burrito. Rosalie ate more slowly and at last, Sage came up for air.

"I'm so sorry I missed the wedding."

"Babe," Rosalie protested, setting down her half-eaten burrito and wrapping Sage in her arms – as close as she could get with Bear monopolizing her lap. "It's not important."

"It *is*," Sage insisted. "A lot of people count their wedding day as one of the most important of their lives, and I missed ours."

"Okay, first of all, you didn't miss anything – it's not like I had the wedding anyway," Rosalie said, a slight smile teasing her lips. "And second, you had a damn good reason."

Ah, there was that precipice. Sage could feel her toes curling over the edge.

"I want to talk to you about that." Really, it was the last thing she wanted to talk about, but they *needed* to discuss it. She braced herself for the freefall. "You've seen me at my worst now, and I can't promise it'll never happen again. I've spent the last year trying to be as normal as humanly possible, manage my symptoms without letting you know I was experiencing them, not let it affect you at all... but I have schizophrenia and I'm going to have it for the rest of my life. I'm not always going to be able to keep it to myself, and I totally understand if you don't want to sign up for that. Now would be a good time, actually, since the wedding–"

Rosalie cut her off, squeezing Sage's hand. "I'm not going anywhere."

"You say that now, but have you *really* thought about it?" Sage pressed. "What if the rest of our lives is like the past week?"

"It won't be," Rosalie said, "because you have a bunch of people in place to support you and help you manage your symptoms. Even if things feel out of whack right now, we'll figure out how to fix them again."

Sage studied her eyes for any trace of uncertainty, but all she saw was love and compassion... Could she be so understanding if the roles were reversed? "You're a saint."

Rosalie laughed. "I just love you. And I don't want you to keep your symptoms to yourself and try to be 'normal' for my sake – I just want you to be yourself because that's who I care about, who I fell in love with."

"Are you sure?" Sage asked. "We've only been together a year. You don't even like bringing me around your dad."

Rosalie's brow furrowed. "What?"

Sage frowned too. "You never wanted me to get to know him. When we had the menu tasting, you steered me to the seat the farthest from him, and you never want me to come along when you meet up with him." Rosalie's mouth opened, and before she could lose the courage to speak her piece, Sage hurried to add, "You don't want him to see the real me."

Rosalie scooped Bear off the middle cushion into her lap and slid into his place, throwing her arms around Sage. "I *love* the real you and that is not the reason. Babe, I'm so sorry I made you think it was."

"What was it, then?"

"It's *him!*" Rosalie was still holding her tight. "And me, and my guilt over how I've handled my relationship with him in the past..."

She sat upright again, taking Sage's hands in her own.

"I told you that he's an alcoholic," she said, and Sage nodded. "What I didn't tell you was how awful it really was growing up with him. I minimized it." She smiled. "Kind of like you minimized your symptoms to keep from scaring me off."

"You thought your dad would scare me off?" Sage asked.

"I *know* he would have," Rosalie said. "Or if not him, you'd see how irritated I can get with him, and how sometimes all I can do is avoid him, and you'd hate me for it the way my aunt does. He made my life a living hell when I was a kid – he was a mean drunk, and I could never guess what was going to set him off. I got the hell out of that house as soon as I could, moved away for college, but then my Aunt Kathy started calling me, asking me how I could leave him when we both knew he couldn't take care of himself."

"What a bitch," Sage grumbled. "She knew, but she

expected a child to take care of her own father, rather than stepping in to help?"

"It hit me right in the gut, though," Rosalie said. "I already felt guilty, and then she was saying it too. And after college, when he was sober and I took a chance on moving back in with him when I got the job at the Gazette, I tried to have a relationship with him again. And it fell apart pretty much immediately. I barely ever see him, and when I do I'm looking for the nearest exit the whole time." She looked into Sage's eyes, her own wide and vulnerable. "I was afraid you would look at my relationship with him and think the exact same thing – how could a daughter treat her sick father like that? What kind of monster acts like that?"

Now Sage threw her arms around Rosalie, squishing Bear happily between them. "I just told you that you're a saint, and I still think so – you're not a monster for trying your best with him and then taking care of yourself."

"And you're not weird or abnormal because of your neurodivergence," Rosalie said. "Life's hard... but it's nothing we can't handle together, right?"

Sage grinned, a genuine smile that stretched across her whole face, for the first time in three days. She breathed deep, and it felt like she was finally on solid ground again. "I love you so goddamn much, Rosalie."

Rosalie laughed. "I love you too, more than anything or anyone."

Bear whined.

"Tied with Bear," she amended.

They kissed, excitement yielding to a long, slow,

yearning embrace. It felt like far more than three days since they'd connected this way, and Sage had been starting to worry that they never would again. This, though... it felt just right.

When Bear finally had enough of being squished between them and jumped down to go gnaw on his favorite ball, Sage took Rosalie's hand. "What happened between you and Casey? You're not fighting because me, are you?"

Rosalie sighed. "We were fighting, but we made up. I'll tell you about it some other time."

Sage nodded. "I do have one more serious thing to discuss with you."

"Yeah?"

"I think we should call off the wedding... or not reschedule it, rather," she said. "I've been afraid to even let myself think about it for the last week, but if you'll still have me, I think we should have the wedding of *our* dreams – not the one Stella's been planning."

Rosalie laughed. "I am one hundred percent with you on that. That wedding was cursed and I shudder to think what our marriage would have been like if we'd gone through with it."

"We don't need Stella energy," Sage agreed.

"So, what's the wedding of our dreams?" Rosalie asked.

Sage smiled. "Glad you asked, because that *has* been percolating in the back of my mind for the last few months..."

37
ROSALIE

The wedding took place at sunset three days later. Sage wore a crisp white linen suit, and she'd insisted that Rosalie buy the vintage dress from the boutique on the pier. Rosalie dyed her hair pink to match Sage's light blue – which had never fully washed out like the jar promised. Having Sage's fingers massaging through Rosalie's hair as she applied the dye was just as much fun as the color itself.

Plus, they both enjoyed the fact that Stella would absolutely hate it if she knew.

She was most definitely not invited, but they had their ring Bear just like they wanted, with a pair of modest but pretty white gold bands tied to a ribbon at his neck. They had Sage's mom, dad and sister, and they had Casey – only the people most important to them, and most supportive.

And they had a hell of a view.

They'd decided to get married on the beach just

beyond the pier, where so many of their best memories had been made. They were barefoot, the sand was warm and comfy without being scorching on Rosalie's soles, and a fresh, salty ocean breeze was coming off the water.

"Well?" Sage asked as the two of them joined hands and turned to face each other, ready to begin the ceremony. "Is this the wedding of your dreams or would you have rather had something more traditional?"

"I can't imagine anything more perfect," Rosalie said.

She nodded to the officiant, who'd been the one flexible, helpful person in the entire wedding planning process. She'd happily agreed to give up an hour of her evening at the last minute, and even did the legwork to check with the city that their beachside wedding could happen like they wanted.

"Friends and family, we are gathered here to join Sage Evans and Rosalie West in loving matrimony," she began.

Rosalie felt the tears welling instantly, the back of her throat getting thick with emotion. When a tear slid down her cheek, Sage reached up and swiped it away with her thumb.

"Are you okay?" she whispered.

Rosalie nodded, and the officiant paused to let them speak. "We've been through so much this past year, and it could have destroyed us, but I like to think it made us stronger."

"It absolutely did," Sage agreed. "We're still standing."

"We're having our wedding, *our* way."

Sage grinned. "I'm marrying the girl of my dreams – that's the only thing that matters."

She leaned in, cupping her hands around Rosalie's cheeks and kissing her sweetly, slowly. Savoring it.

Behind them, the officiant said, "I'd say it's not time for that yet, but you do you."

Their newly combined family laughed, and at last, Rosalie turned to the officiant. "Okay, marry us please. I don't want to wait another second."

After the ceremony, Willow suggested going up on the pier for a traditional wedding feast of coney dogs and funnel cakes. Food was pretty much the farthest thing from Rosalie's mind, and she could see from the look in Sage's eyes that she was in agreement.

Thankfully, Casey was back in sync with them and she could see it too. She reached for Bear's leash, saying, "Hand him over. I'm ready to play dogsitter while you two go have your own celebration."

"I'll eat coney dogs in your honor," Sage's dad promised with a cheeky smile, and Angela smacked his arm.

"Three coney dogs? I think not."

"Four," Scott said, "I was counting the dog."

"Oh, Bear is getting a coney dog," Casey said. "It's his big day too – his mommies got married."

The little group drifted off in two different directions, most of them heading for the food stalls on the pier,

Rosalie and Sage heading up the beach instead. There was an old, well-kept hotel within walking distance, and Rosalie had sprung for a room to make the night a little more special than going back to their apartment.

It was small but elegant, with an ornate iron bedframe and vintage damask wallpaper. Not that Rosalie had eyes for any of those details – she took them in as background noise as she pulled Sage to her at the foot of the bed.

"You have no idea how proud and lucky and fucking *horny* I am to call you my wife."

"I brought something along to help you with that," Sage winked, setting down the backpack they'd brought with clothes for the morning. "But first, I have a wedding gift for you."

"You're my wedding gift," Rosalie protested.

Sage unzipped the bag and carefully unwrapped the bundle of clothes within. At the center was a glass rose, and Rosalie gasped.

"You made me a new one."

"If you recall, I actually promised to make you a hundred new ones," Sage said, picking it up and holding it out to her. "Life kind of got in the way this year and I fell short of that goal just a little bit."

"I don't care," Rosalie said. "It's beautiful."

It was more intricate and delicate than the first one. Sage had learned from the first iteration, and with everything she made, her glassblowing skills improved tenfold. Rosalie turned it in awe, watching it catch the light from the floor lamp nearby.

"I made a cloche for it too," Sage explained. "That's back at the apartment, I figured it wouldn't travel well. But I wanted to make something you could display it in."

"And that will keep it safe from Bear," Rosalie chuckled.

Sage winked. "That definitely crossed my mind."

Rosalie set the rose down on the top of the dresser, carefully far from the edge. Then she turned back to Sage. "I don't mean to be greedy, but you mentioned something to help my... condition?"

"Your horniness," Sage grinned.

"Yes." Rosalie looked at the backpack. "What have you got in there?"

Sage rooted around beneath their clothes and found what she was looking for. She produced a familiar red leather harness, and if Rosalie wasn't already hot and wet with desire, she would have gushed with need right then and there. She bit her lip in anticipation as she watched Sage produce a soft silicone strap-on and wiggle it teasingly.

"What do you think?"

"I think I couldn't ask for a more perfect wife."

"I *know* I couldn't," Sage answered. She tossed the strap-on and harness on the bed, swept the bag with their clothes to the floor, then put her hands on Rosalie's shoulders and spun her around.

Rosalie let out a giggle, then a shiver rolled down her spine as she felt Sage's fingers working their way through the laces and clasps of her antique gown. She stripped it off her as fast as she could, which wasn't nearly fast enough for Rosalie's pounding heart. She felt the cap sleeves sliding down her shoulders, and Sage's hands fisting in the material at her hips.

Rosalie wore a lacy, pure white bra and panties beneath it, and Sage didn't even take the time to see her in them. She just unclasped the bra and threw it to the side, then pulled Rosalie's panties down to her ankles. Rosalie was about to turn to face her when Sage grabbed the nape of her neck and pushed her forward, palms flat on the mattress in front of her.

"This is new," Rosalie commented with another pleasant shiver.

"We may be married now, but we still have a whole lot of firsts left ahead of us," Sage said, wrapping one arm around Rosalie's hip and sliding her fingers between her thighs. "You're so wet, baby."

"Make love to me," Rosalie said. She grinned and added, "Then fuck me hard, and then make love to me again."

"All night long," Sage promised. She bent forward and kissed her way down Rosalie's back, and when she could feel her quivering beneath her, she plunged her fingers into Rosalie's core.

The sensation was overwhelming. Rosalie's arms gave out and she collapsed on the bed. Sage guided her down to her knees, her arms stretched out in front of her and her hands grasping the blankets. Sage brought her other hand around Rosalie's body, using the slickness between her folds to lubricate her clit and then thrusting her fingers back into her.

"Does that feel good?"

"My eyes are rolling back in my head," Rosalie said, and Sage growled in satisfaction.

"I'm going to make you come so hard, so many fucking times."

She thrust inside her, hips connecting lustily with Rosalie's backside as her fingers played over her clit and between her folds. It was all Rosalie could do to hang onto the bedsheets like they were anchoring her to this world, and it wasn't long before she was coming just as hard as Sage promised against her hand.

She turned her head to scream into the mattress and Sage lowered her mouth to Rosalie's ear. "Let me hear you, please, baby."

So Rosalie gave herself over to the orgasm, her entire body clenching and pulsing and writhing with zero input from her brain, god knew what coming out of her mouth as Sage's fingers fucked her deep and hard.

When Rosalie finally caught her breath again, Sage kissed her neck, just below the ear, then stood up to undress herself. Rosalie rolled onto her back, trying to regain muscle control to little avail. All she managed to do was prop herself on her elbows, enjoying the little strip show Sage was giving her as her tie and then her pants and finally her button-down shirt came off.

"Your turn," Rosalie said, holding out her hand once Sage was naked before her. "I wanna make you come like that."

Sage just shook her head. "Later. First, I get to have my way with you."

CARA MALONE

She reached for the strap-on and suddenly Rosalie was throbbing with need all over again. She spread her legs wide, displaying herself for Sage and teasing her fingers through her own wetness as she watched Sage step into the harness.

"Fuck, I think you're the one who's toying with me," she said through gritted teeth. "Do you have any idea how sexy you are?"

"Do you know how sexy *you* are?" Rosalie shot back, letting her eyes sweep over every inch of her wife's body – the firmness of her biceps and the slight softness of her belly, the look of hunger in her eyes and hard little pebbles of her nipples. And the silicone cock jutting out from her hips, ready and eager to drive Rosalie out of her mind.

Sage knelt on the bed and Rosalie scooted up it, making room for her. Sage wrapped her hand around the strap-on, pointing it toward Rosalie's pussy and sliding it up and down through her folds to get it good and wet.

"Hard or slow?" Sage asked.

Rosalie smiled. "Yes."

"Yes, ma'am," Sage said, then pressed into her. She fucked Rosalie just like she asked, with long, slow strokes that hit deep inside her, the contact of their hips meeting with every penetration sending little jolts through her clit.

"Just like that," Rosalie nodded, clinging to Sage.

Before long, the sensations were building in her, any sensitivity from her last orgasm dissipated and only longing remaining.

"Faster," she breathed.

"Are you getting close again?" Sage asked.

"Yes. Your body feels so good." She was holding Sage so tight it was probably hard for her to get any leverage, but all Rosalie wanted was to be as close to her as possible. As close as any two people could be. "Can you come with me?"

Sage squirmed her hand down between them and then Rosalie felt vibration between her legs. She shuddered with a pre-orgasm contraction and forced herself to let go of Sage so she could move more freely.

"Fuck me, baby. Fuck me hard."

With a grin, Sage braced herself with her hands on either side of Rosalie's shoulders and quickened her pace. Rosalie watched the expression on her wife's face morph from the desire to please her to an imperative to chase after her own pleasure as it built inside her.

Rosalie bucked her hips up to meet each of Sage's thrusts, the addition of the vibration sending her over the edge in short order. It took Sage a few more seconds, grinding against the clit-stimulating base of the vibrator, before she joined Rosalie in ecstasy. She lost all control of her rhythm, bucking into her however she could to chase that delirious pleasure, and somehow, that sent Rosalie even higher, a third orgasm quickly following the second.

When they were both lying on their backs, panting and sweaty with exertion, Rosalie rolled her head to the side to look at her wife. "Told you I wanted to make you come next."

Sage just shrugged. "Happy wife, happy life."

EPILOGUE – SAGE

ONE YEAR LATER

S age woke out of a dead sleep to an alarm screaming in her ear and a dog's cool, wet nose nudging her jaw. It was three a.m. and she felt like she was swimming up through quicksand into consciousness, but before she was even fully alert, there was a smile on her face.

"Babe, it's time," she mumbled, reaching for her alarm.

Then Rosalie was curling up around her, nuzzling in on the other side of her neck and kissing her awake. "Happy anniversary, Ssage."

She laughed. They still used her accidental nickname from time to time, and they'd made two wedding scrapbooks in the past year – one to commemorate the actual event, and one to memorialize every little disaster that had happened along the way.

"Happy anniversary." Sage kissed her. "Are you ready to spend a whole day traveling?"

"I can't wait," Rosalie said, sliding out of bed. "I'm gonna make a quick pot of coffee."

She slid out of bed and Bear trailed after her. Sage forced herself upright lest she fall back asleep. She'd worked closely with Dr. Khan after the wedding to get her medication mix just right again and things with her mental health had been going smoothly. It meant being extra-vigilant not to skip any more doses, even on nights when she knew she'd have to get up early, but it was worth it.

She could pass out again the minute her butt hit the plane seat – they had a ten-hour flight to Amsterdam that lifted off in two hours.

It took an extra year, but Sage had finally made their dream honeymoon happen. For the next week and a half, they were going to explore the canals and museums of Amsterdam, the unique architecture of Rotterdam, the picturesque countryside with its iconic tulip fields. Sage had made time in the trip to meet up with some of Rosalie's distant relatives, and of course, lots of time to just be together, wherever the days took them.

Sage's dad came and drove them to the airport, and took Bear to stay with him and Angela until they were back. They had seats in coach, which were cramped and uncomfortable but also the best they could afford. It was more important to have cash for the journey, so they could explore everything they wanted to see in the Netherlands. A little leg cramping in the meantime was a small price to pay.

Not that Sage noticed. She fell asleep somewhere

over the Atlantic and woke up about an hour before their arrival. There was green land beneath them again, and wispy clouds outside her window.

"How long have I been out?" she asked, wiping the sleep from her eyes.

"Basically the whole flight," Rosalie said with a laugh. "I read a book from cover to cover."

"Shit, I'm sorry." Sage had visions of the night they took Bear to the emergency vet, the guilt she'd felt for not being fully present for Rosalie and Bear. It didn't feel good.

"Don't worry about it," Rosalie said, squeezing her into a side hug, the best she could manage in their side-by-side seats. "It was a really good book."

"Oh yeah? Tell me about it."

Rosalie gave Sage a detailed summary of the historical fiction she'd been reading that took them all the way up to the airplane's descent. They gathered their bags – they'd traveled light, and Sage had made sure to keep her medication with her in her carryon – and found a taxi to their hotel.

It was a beautiful stone building and their room overlooked one of the canals. It was ten p.m. local time, but the sun was only just setting and Rosalie pulled Sage over to the window to watch it.

Sage wrapped her arms around Rosalie's waist, and Rosalie laid her head on Sage's shoulder. "Thank you so much for making this happen. I love it here already."

"It is beautiful," Sage agreed. "But I'd love anything as long as I got to experience it with you."

The End

In the mood for another romcom? Check out Good Vibes, a sapphic romantic comedy about finding love and self-acceptance in the strangest places.

Read it in Kindle Unlimited